1st EDITION

Perspectives on Modern World History

The *Brown v. Board of Education* Trial

1st EDITION

Perspectives on Modern World History

The *Brown v. Board of Education* Trial

Julia Garbus

Editor

GREENHAVEN PRESS

A part of Gale, Cengage Learning

GALE CENGAGE Learning

Farmington Hills, Mich • San Francisco • New York • Waterville, Maine
Meriden, Conn • Mason, Ohio • Chicago

GALE
CENGAGE Learning

Elizabeth Des Chenes, *Director, Content Strategy*
Douglas Dentino, *Manager, New Product*

WCN: 01-100-101

For more information, contact:
Greenhaven Press
27500 Drake Rd.
Farmington Hills, MI 48331-3535
Or you can visit our Internet site at gale.cengage.com.

Articles in Greenhaven Press anthologies are often edited for length to meet page requirements. In addition, original titles of these works are changed to clearly present the main thesis and to explicitly indicate the author's opinion. Every effort is made to ensure that Greenhaven Press accurately reflects the original intent of the authors. Every effort has been made to trace the owners of copyrighted material.

LIBRARY OF CONGRESS CATALOGING-IN-PUBLICATION DATA

The Brown v. Board of Education Trial / edited by Julia Garbus.
pages cm -- (Perspectives on modern world history)
Summary: "Perspectives on Modern World History: The Brown v. Board of Education Trial: The series provides basic historical information on a significant event in modern world history, presents the controversies surrounding the event, and provides first-person narratives"-- Provided by publisher.
Includes bibliographical references and index.
ISBN 978-0-7377-7307-1 (hardback)
1. Brown, Oliver, 1918-1961--Trials, litigation, etc.--Juvenile literature. 2. Topeka (Kan.). Board of Education--Trials, litigation, etc.--Juvenile literature. 3. Segregation in education--Law and legislation--United States--Juvenile literature. 4. African Americans--Civil rights--Juvenile literature. I. Garbus, Julia, editor.
KF228.B76B77 2014
344.73'0798--dc23

2014020505

Printed in the United States of America
1 2 3 4 5 6 7 18 17 16 15 14

CONTENTS

FOREWORD

> *"History cannot give us a program for the future, but it can give us a fuller understanding of ourselves, and of our common humanity, so that we can better face the future."*
>
> *—Robert Penn Warren, American poet and novelist*

The history of each nation is punctuated by momentous events that represent turning points for that nation, with an impact felt far beyond its borders. These events—displaying the full range of human capabilities, from violence, greed, and ignorance to heroism, courage, and strength—are nearly always complicated and multifaceted. Any student of history faces the challenge of grasping the many strands that constitute such world-changing events as wars, social movements, and environmental disasters. But understanding these significant historic events can be enhanced by exposure to a variety of perspectives, whether of people involved intimately or of ones observing from a distance of miles or years. Understanding can also be increased by learning about the controversies surrounding such events and exploring hot-button issues from multiple angles. Finally, true understanding of important historic events involves knowledge of the events' human impact—of the ways such events affected people in their everyday lives—all over the world.

Perspectives on Modern World History examines global historic events from the twentieth century onward by presenting analysis and observation from numerous vantage points. Each volume offers high school, early college level, and general interest readers a thematically arranged anthology of previously published materials that address a major historical event, with an emphasis on international coverage. Each volume opens with background information on the event, then presents the controversies surrounding that event, and concludes with first-person narratives from people who lived through the event or were affected by it. By providing primary sources from the time of the event, as well as relevant commentary surrounding the event, this series can be used to inform debate, help develop critical thinking skills, increase global awareness, and enhance an understanding of international perspectives on history.

Material in each volume is selected from a diverse range of sources, including journals, magazines, newspapers, nonfiction books, personal narratives, speeches, congressional testimony, government documents, pamphlets, organization newsletters, and position papers. Articles taken from these sources are carefully edited and introduced to provide context and background. Each volume of Perspectives on Modern World History includes an array of views on events of global significance. Much of the material comes from international sources and from US sources that provide extensive international coverage.

Each volume in the Perspectives on Modern World History series also includes:

- A full-color **world map**, offering context and geographic perspective.
- An annotated **table of contents** that provides a brief summary of each essay in the volume.
- An **introduction** specific to the volume topic.
- For each viewpoint, a brief **introduction** that has notes about the author and source of the viewpoint, and that provides a summary of its main points.
- Full-color **charts, graphs, maps**, and other visual representations.

- Informational **sidebars** that explore the lives of key individuals, give background on historical events, or explain scientific or technical concepts.
- A **glossary** that defines key terms, as needed.
- A **chronology** of important dates preceding, during, and immediately following the event.
- A **bibliography** of additional books, periodicals, and websites for further research.
- A comprehensive **subject index** that offers access to people, places, and events cited in the text.

Perspectives on Modern World History is designed for a broad spectrum of readers who want to learn more about not only history but also current events, political science, government, international relations, and sociology—students doing research for class assignments or debates, teachers and faculty seeking to supplement course materials, and others wanting to improve their understanding of history. Each volume of Perspectives on Modern World History is designed to illuminate a complicated event, to spark debate, and to show the human perspective behind the world's most significant happenings of recent decades.

INTRODUCTION

Clarendon County, South Carolina, 1947. African American children walk miles to their rundown school, going in shifts so the tiny building can accommodate all of the area's students. Their families collect wood for the school's wood stoves. High school students take only four classes because their hand-me-down textbooks cover only those subjects. As the children walk, white students pass them on buses, headed to their own "modern, safe, sanitary, well-equipped, lighted, and healthy" schools.[1] State law requires this segregation: "Separate schools shall be provided for children of the white and colored races, and no child of either race shall be permitted to attend a school provided for children of the other race."[2] Fed up with the substandard conditions their children face, twenty-two black families band together to challenge the South Carolina law.

The South had been segregated since shortly after the Thirteenth Amendment made slavery unconstitutional in 1865. Three years later, Congress passed the Fourteenth Amendment to guarantee rights for freed slaves; it specifies that no state shall deprive a person of "the due process of law" or of the "equal protection of the law." Despite the amendment, southern states drew up laws, known as "Jim Crow laws," which mandated segregation in public places, transportation, and schools and in all restaurants and restrooms. In 1896 the US Supreme Court heard a case challenging these laws. Homer Plessy, a black man, was arrested for sitting in a train coach reserved for whites. He sued, arguing that train segregation violated the Fourteenth Amendment's equal protection clause. The Supreme Court disagreed. In *Plessy v. Ferguson* (1896), it held that although the

Fourteenth Amendment guaranteed *legal* equality of the races, the amendment "could not have been intended to abolish distinctions based upon color, or to endorse social, rather than political, equality."[3] Railroad companies were to provide "equal, but separate" accommodations for black and white passengers. "Separate but equal" would continue to be the law of the land for over fifty years—until the landmark Supreme Court case *Brown v. Board of Education* (1954).

African Americans refused to buckle under. The National Association for the Advancement of Colored People (NAACP) was founded in 1909 to work for political, economic, and social equality. In 1930 the group began planning a legal attack on segregation. The US legal system is based on precedent: courts' rulings in earlier cases about the same topic must be followed. Therefore NAACP lawyers mapped out a series of cases that would become the precedents to dismantle segregation in the public schools. The legal team decided to first attack law and graduate school segregation, because there was no place in the South where African Americans could receive a PhD or a degree from an accredited law school. African American attorney Thurgood Marshall spearheaded NAACP's legal team. Refused admission to the University of Maryland's law school because of his race, Marshall had become the top student at the all-black Howard University law school.

The NAACP's first challenge to segregation at the Supreme Court came in *State of Missouri ex rel Gaines v. Canada* in 1938. The case involved Lloyd Gaines, a black man seeking to attend the all-white University of Missouri law school. In its decision, the Supreme Court held that the equal protection clause required the state to provide Gaines a legal education within its borders. In 1950 the state of Texas set up a one-person "black" law school in a basement rather than admitting Heman Sweatt to the University of Texas School of Law.

The Supreme Court held in *Sweatt v. Painter* that this separate law school would not provide Sweatt an equal education and ordered him admitted to Texas. Neighboring Oklahoma did admit African American applicant George McLaurin to a PhD program, but required him to sit in the classroom doorway and at a separate lunch table. The court held that "appellant, being admitted to a state-supported graduate school, must receive the same treatment at the hands of the state as students of other races."[4] State-supported segregation in graduate and professional schools was over, and the NAACP had laid the groundwork for a direct legal challenge to segregation in public schools.

The NAACP filed cases in five different states challenging segregation at the primary, middle, and high school levels. One was the Clarendon County, South Carolina, case *Briggs v. Elliott.* In Virginia, high school student Barbara Johns had led a student strike to demand better conditions in her all-black high school, where 450 students were jammed into tar-paper shacks heated with pot-bellied stoves; this case became *Davis v. County School Board of Prince Edward County*. Parents in Delaware (*Belton (Bulah) v. Gebhart*) and Washington, DC (*Bolling v. Sharpe*) brought cases as well. The Supreme Court consolidated all the cases together under the name of the case involving Topeka, Kansas, elementary schools: *Brown v. Board of Education*. On May 17, 1954, the Supreme Court handed down its unanimous opinion: "We conclude that in the field of public education the doctrine of 'separate but equal' has no place. Separate educational facilities are inherently unequal."

The *Brown* decision sparked the civil rights movement. The year after the decision, Rosa Parks' refusal to give up her bus seat launched the Montgomery Bus Boycott led by Martin Luther King Jr. Nonviolent protest and civil disobedience, boycotts, sit-ins, and marches by African Americans and white allies led to the passage of the

Civil Rights Act of 1964, banning discrimination based on race, color, religion, or national origin in employment practices and public accommodations; the Voting Rights Act of 1965; and the Fair Housing Act of 1968.

But as civil rights advocates celebrated the ruling and fought for equal treatment in other arenas, the South revolted. A group of 101 southern congressmen signed a "Southern Manifesto" vowing their opposition. One senator termed the proper strategy "massive resistance." The Supreme Court's decision that desegregation should proceed "with all deliberate speed"[5] was vague enough to allow southern states to balk, stall, and rebel. For example, Prince Edward County, the location of the *Davis* case, shut down its public schools for five years rather than desegregate. The governor of Arkansas ordered the state National Guard to prevent nine African American students from attending a previously all-white high school, forcing President Dwight D. Eisenhower to send in the 101st Airborne Division to guarantee the students' safety. Ten years after the *Brown* decision, only one-fiftieth of African American children in the South attended integrated schools.[6] Many students in the North, too, attended schools segregated *de facto* (in fact, as opposed to segregation *de jure*—by law—as had existed in the South).

Finally, in 1969, the court made clear that time was up. "There is no longer the slightest excuse, reason, or justification for further postponement of the time when every public school system in the United States should be a unitary one,"[7] declared Justice Hugo Black, writing for a court that now included African American justice Thurgood Marshall. The court began overseeing desegregation in both the South and the North, ordering busing and other tools to overcome residential segregation caused by "white flight" to the suburbs. After turnover on the court led to a more conservative majority in the 1990s, however, the court stopped supporting court-ordered remedies for segregation. Segregation has increased since.

In *Perspectives in Modern World History: The* Brown v. Board of Education *Trial*, readers will hear the voices of people involved with the case—from the brave teens who first integrated schools after the *Brown* ruling to the politicians fighting to keep segregation alive. The following chapters explore controversies about *Brown*'s interpretation, its implementation, and its short and long-term effects, both in the United States and abroad. This volume will give readers the background to join the debate about what "equal protection under the law" might mean for the twenty-first century.

Notes

1. Harry Briggs et al., "Petition to the Board of Trustees for School District No. 22," November 11, 1949, p. 2. Series L14167, Complaints Files, 1948–1951. Records of the Clarendon County Board of Education at the South Carolina Department of Archives and History.
2. South Carolina Constitution of 1985, article 11, § 7.
3. Henry Billings Brown, Opinion, *Plessy v. Ferguson*, US Supreme Court, May 18, 1896.
4. Fred M. Vinson, Opinion, *McLaurin v. Oklahoma State Regents for Higher Education et al.*, US Supreme Court, June 5, 1950.
5. Earl Warren, Opinion, *Brown v. Board of Education of Topeka (Brown II)*, US Supreme Court, May 31, 1955.
6. James Anderson and Dara N. Burne, eds., *The Unfinished Agenda of Brown v. Board of Education*. Hoboken, NJ: John Wiley and Sons, 2004, p. 53.
7. Hugo Black, Opinion, *Alexander v. Holmes County Board of Education*, US Supreme Court, September 5, 1969.

World Map

160°W
140°W
120°W
100°W
80°W
60°W
80°N
60°N
40°N
20°N
0°
20°S
40°S
60°S
80°S
40°W
Alaska (U.S.)
CANADA
UNITED STATES
ATLANTIC OCEAN
MEXICO
Tropic of Cancer
see inset below
Hawaii (U.S.)
PACIFIC OCEAN
Equator
Line Islands (U.S.)
Galápagos Islands (Ecuador)
COLOMBIA
French Guiana (France)
SURINAME
ECUADOR
PERU
BRAZIL
BOLIVIA
American Samoa (U.S.)
SAMOA
French Polynesia (France)
TONGA
Pitcairn Islands (U.K.)
Tropic of Capricorn
PARAGUAY
CHILE
URUGUAY
ARGENTINA
Falkland Islands (U.K.)
SOUTHERN OCEAN
Antarctic Circle
90°W
85°W
80°W
75°W
60°W
25°N
20°N
15°N
10°N
Gulf of Mexico
N
UNITED STATES
BAHAMAS
Tropic of Cancer
CUBA
Turks and Caicos Islands (U.K.)
U.S. Virgin Islands (U.S.)
British Virgin Islands (U.K.)
Anguilla (U.K.)
St. Martin (St. Maarten) (France & Neth. Antilles)
ANTIGUA AND BARBUDA
MEXICO
HAITI
Cayman Islands (U.K.)
Puerto Rico (U.S.)
ST. KITTS AND NEVIS
Montserrat (U.K.)
Guadeloupe (France)
DOMINICA
BELIZE
JAMAICA
DOMINICAN REPUBLIC
GUATEMALA
Caribbean Sea
Martinique (France)
HONDURAS
ST. LUCIA
BARBADOS
EL SALVADOR
ST. VINCENT AND THE GRENADINES
GRENADA
NICARAGUA
0 200 400 mi.
0 200 400 km
Aruba (Neth.)
Netherlands Antilles (Neth.)
TRINIDAD AND TOBAGO
Lake Maracaibo
COSTA RICA
PACIFIC OCEAN
PANAMA
VENEZUELA
GUYANA
COLOMBIA

ARCTIC OCEAN
see inset below
Arctic Circle
RUSSIA
KAZAKHSTAN
MONGOLIA
GEORGIA
AZER.
ARMENIA
UZBEK.
TURKMEN.
KYRGYZSTAN
TAJIKISTAN
CHINA
NORTH KOREA
SOUTH KOREA
JAPAN
PACIFIC OCEAN
ISRAEL
IRAQ
IRAN
AFGHAN.
JORDAN
BAHRAIN
PAKISTAN
NEPAL
BHUTAN
KUWAIT
QATAR
ALGERIA
LIBYA
EGYPT
SAUDI ARABIA
U.A.E.
OMAN
INDIA
MYANMAR (BURMA)
BANGLADESH
TAIWAN (Claimed by China)
LAOS
THAILAND
VIETNAM
CAMBODIA
PHILIPPINES
MARSHALL ISLANDS
ERITREA
YEMEN
CHAD
SUDAN
DJIBOUTI
ETHIOPIA
CEN. AFR. REP.
CAMEROON
SOMALIA
SRI LANKA
BRUNEI
MALAYSIA
SINGAPORE
FEDERATED STATES OF MICRONESIA
KIRIBATI
DEM. REP. OF THE CONGO
UGANDA
KENYA
RWANDA
BURUNDI
TANZANIA
GABON
CONGO
SÃO TOMÉ AND PRÍNCIPE
MALDIVES
INDONESIA
NAURU
PAPUA NEW GUINEA
SOLOMON ISLANDS
TIMOR-LESTE
TUVALU
SEYCHELLES
COMOROS
INDIAN OCEAN
ATLANTIC OCEAN
ANGOLA
MALAWI
ZAMBIA
MOZAMBIQUE
FIJI ISLANDS
VANUATU
MADAGASCAR
MAURITIUS
Réunion (France)
ZIMBABWE
BOTSWANA
NAMIBIA
New Caledonia (France)
AUSTRALIA
SOUTH AFRICA
SWAZILAND
LESOTHO
0 1000 2000 mi.
0 1000 2000 km
NEW ZEALAND
N
SOUTHERN OCEAN
ANTARCTICA

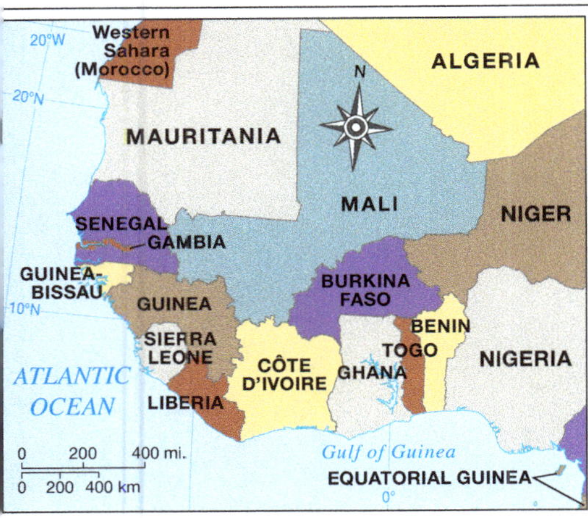

Western Sahara (Morocco)
ALGERIA
MAURITANIA
N
MALI
NIGER
SENEGAL
GAMBIA
GUINEA-BISSAU
GUINEA
BURKINA FASO
BENIN
SIERRA LEONE
TOGO
NIGERIA
CÔTE D'IVOIRE
GHANA
ATLANTIC OCEAN
LIBERIA
0 200 400 mi.
0 200 400 km
Gulf of Guinea
EQUATORIAL GUINEA

N
SWEDEN
FINLAND
NORWAY
0 200 400 mi.
0 200 400 km
ESTONIA
North Sea
DENMARK
IRELAND
UNITED KINGDOM
LATVIA
RUSSIA
Baltic Sea
LITHUANIA
RUSSIA
NETHERLANDS
BELARUS
ATLANTIC OCEAN
GERMANY
POLAND
BELGIUM
LUX.
CZECH REP.
UKRAINE
Bay of Biscay
FRANCE
LIECH.
SLOVAKIA
MOLDOVA
SWITZ.
AUSTRIA
HUNGARY
SLOVENIA
ROMANIA
CROATIA
ANDORRA
MONACO
ITALY
BOS. AND HERZ.
SERBIA
Black Sea
PORTUGAL
SAN MARINO
MONT.
BULGARIA
SPAIN
Corsica (France)
MAC.
Sardinia (Italy)
VATICAN CITY
ALBANIA
Gibraltar (U.K.)
Balearic Isands (Spain)
TURKEY
Ceuta (Spain)
Melilla (Spain)
Sicily (Italy)
GREECE
MALTA
CYPRUS
SYRIA
MOROCCO
ALGERIA
TUNISIA
Mediterranean Sea
Crete (Greece)
LEBANON

CHAPTER 1

Historical Background on the *Brown v. Board of Education* Trial

VIEWPOINT 1

The Road to the Landmark *Brown* Court Rulings

West's Encyclopedia of American Law

The following viewpoint reviews the history of the 1954 US Supreme Court case *Brown v. Board of Education*. The authors explain that the roots of the struggle to end segregation date back to Jim Crow laws enacted in the South following Reconstruction and the abolition of slavery. The *Brown* case reversed the decision in the infamous *Plessy v. Ferguson* case (1896), which upheld racial segregation. The National Association for the Advancement of Colored People (NAACP) spearheaded the successful legal challenge to the *Plessy* ruling. In 1952 two school segregation cases were brought to the Supreme Court by Thurgood Marshall, then the head of the NAACP legal branch. The authors also note that the court's 1954 decision in *Brown* and its subsequent 1955 decision *Brown II* changed race relations in the United States and helped in future efforts against racial discrimination. *West's*

Photo on opposite page: Thurgood Marshall discusses the landmark *Brown v. Board of Education* trial in front of the US Supreme Court building in August 1958. **© Ed Clark/Time Life Pictures/Getty Images.**

SOURCE. "Brown v. Board of Education of Topeka, Kansas," *West's Encyclopedia of American Law*, 2nd. ed., vol. 2, Shirelle Phelps and Jeffrey Lehman, eds. Detroit: Gale, 2005, pp. 142–147. Copyright © 2004 Cengage Learning.

Encyclopedia of American Law is a comprehensive overview of events and cases that are significant to US law. Shirelle Phelps and Jeffrey Lehman are the editors of the multivolume encyclopedia as well as a number of other books about US history, law, and biography.

Brown v. Board of Education was the most significant of a series of judicial decisions overturning segregation laws—laws that separate whites and blacks. Reversing its 1896 decision in *Plessy v. Ferguson*, which established the "separate-but-equal" doctrine that found racial segregation to be constitutional, the Court unanimously decided in *Brown* that laws separating children by race in different schools violated the equal protection clause of the fourteenth amendment, which provides that "[n]o state shall . . . deny to any person . . . the equal protection of the laws." In making its decision, the Court declared that "separate educational facilities are inherently unequal." Moreover, the Court found that segregated schools promote in African American children a harmful and irreparable sense of inferiority that damages not only their lives but the welfare of U.S. society as a whole.

The principle expressed in *Brown* was used in later decisions of the Supreme Court and lower federal courts to reverse segregation in other fields as well. By the end of the 1960s, laws that had required racial segregation in buses, trains, bathrooms, and other public places had been overturned, as had many other laws that obstructed the rights of African Americans. *Brown* thus served as a milestone in the struggle of African Americans to gain equal civil rights in U.S. society. It also symbolized the judicial activism of

> *Brown* was actually the culmination of a decades-long struggle by both African Americans and sympathetic whites against segregation and other discriminatory laws.

the Supreme Court under Chief Justice Earl Warren, who would go on to lead the Court until 1969 in a remarkable era of change with regard to civil rights.

The Painful Legacy of Jim Crow

Brown was actually the culmination of a decades-long struggle by both African Americans and sympathetic whites against segregation and other discriminatory laws. Though it is a given in the early 2000s that persons of all races should enjoy equality under the law in the United States, that has not been the case for most of the country's history. Even after the Civil War had ended and the Thirteenth and Fourteenth Amendments had outlawed slavery and guaranteed the civil rights of "all persons born or naturalized in the United States" (U.S. Const. amend. XIV), southern states and localities established the racially discriminatory Jim Crow laws—also known as the Black Codes—to keep African Americans from enjoying legal equality with whites. The term *Jim Crow* derives from a popular minstrel song of the nineteenth century. These laws made it difficult or impossible for African Americans to vote, made it illegal for them to use the same public facilities as whites, restricted their travel, forbade interracial marriage, and otherwise attempted to keep African Americans in a state of dependence and inferiority with regard to whites. Most of these laws were passed after the Reconstruction period following the Civil War, when the military occupation of the South had ended and the radical wing of the Republican Party, which under President Abraham Lincoln had been instrumental in dismantling slavery, had declined in power. By the mid-1870s, southern whites were again in political control of their region, and many quickly sought to return blacks to a position of legal inferiority through passage of discriminatory laws.

In 1896 the legal standing of the Jim Crow laws was strengthened when, in *Plessy v. Ferguson*, the Supreme

Court upheld the constitutionality of a Louisiana statute requiring blacks and whites to occupy separate railway cars. The law in question, according to the Court, was not a violation of the Equal Protection Clause of the Fourteenth Amendment as long as the facilities provided for each race were separate but equal. Moreover, the Court voiced its disagreement with attempts to challenge segregation laws and with the ideas critics of segregation used to support those challenges. For example, in its opinion, the Court considered it a "fallacy" that "the enforced separation of the two races stamps the colored race with a badge of inferiority," and it scoffed at the notion that "social prejudices may be overcome by legislation." Ironically, the Court reinforced its decision to uphold the legality of segregation on rail cars by noting the existence of laws "requiring separate schools for colored children." The *Plessy* decision and its separate-but-equal doctrine were later used to uphold segregation in public schools and other public facilities.

The NAACP Leads the Charge Against *Plessy*

African Americans and others who sympathized with their cause were bitterly disappointed by the *Plessy* decision. Over a decade later, in 1909, some blacks and whites joined together to form the National Association for the Advancement of Colored People (NAACP), which would eventually coordinate a successful legal challenge to the *Plessy* ruling. The NAACP brought together people of all races in an effort to improve the situation of people of color. Although the NAACP achieved some victories in the fight against Jim Crow laws in the first two decades of its existence, it was not until 1935 that the organization began actively to mount a campaign against segregation in schools. It did so assisted by legal counsels Charles Houston and William H. Hastie, and a young assistant, Thurgood Marshall, who would

Students participate in a geography lesson at a segregated African American school in October 1938. © **Afro American Newspapers/ Gado/Getty Images.**

go on to be a member of the Supreme Court from 1967 to 1991.

By 1939, Marshall had become head of the NAACP legal branch, the NAACP Legal Defense Fund, and by the early 1950s, he and his organization had argued and secured significant legal victories before the Supreme Court that helped set the stage for *Brown*. In *Sweatt v. Painter* (1950), the Court sided with the NAACP Legal Defense Fund when it ruled that a separate law school for blacks in Texas could not provide an education equal to that available to whites at the more established University of Texas Law School. And in another case brought by Marshall's organization, *McLaurin v. Oklahoma State Regents* (1950), the Court ruled that separate library and lecture hall seats for a single black graduate student were a violation of the Fourteenth Amendment. However, neither case addressed the separate-but-equal doctrine of *Plessy*.

Thurgood Marshall's Role

In 1952 Marshall and the NAACP Legal Defense Fund brought two more significant cases to the Supreme Court: *Bolling v. Sharpe* (1954), which dealt with racial segregation of schools in the District of Columbia, and *Brown*, which was actually a consolidation of four class action suits (suits brought to court on behalf of a group of people) from federal district courts in Delaware, Kansas, South Carolina, and Virginia. The NAACP Legal Defense Fund brought the cases to court on behalf of African American children who were refused admission to schools attended by white children as a result of laws allowing or requiring racial segregation in schools. The plaintiff named in the case, Oliver Brown, had a daughter, Linda Brown, who had been denied admission to an all-white elementary school in Topeka, Kansas, because she was black. In all but the Delaware case, a three-judge federal district court had decided against the African American children and in favor of the school districts, citing as precedent the *Plessy* separate-but-equal doctrine. In the Delaware case, the state supreme court also upheld this doctrine but ordered that black children be sent to superior white schools until schools provided for blacks could be improved to an equal condition.

> "[Thurgood Marshall] maintained that a decision in favor of segregation would effectively be a decision to keep African Americans as near as possible to their former state of slavery"

Brown was argued before the Court in 1952 and reargued in 1953. Marshall, in making his statement before the Court, argued that the statutes in question in this case were equivalent to the black codes. He pointed out the contradictions in allowing blacks and whites to vote in the same places and attend the same colleges and universities, but not allowing black and white children to attend the same elementary schools. He also maintained that a decision in favor of segregation would effectively

Oliver Brown: The Name Behind *Brown v. Board of Education*

The Brown of *Brown v. Board of Education of Topeka* is Oliver Brown. Oliver Brown and his daughter, Linda, are remembered today, while the thirty-three plaintiffs, including thirteen parents and twenty children are largely forgotten, simply because Oliver Brown was listed first in the complaint. Had Oliver not agreed to participate in the suit, students today might talk of the famous case, say, of *Carper v. Board of Education* or *Fleming v. Board of Education* (two of the other adult plaintiffs who challenged Topeka's policy). Oliver Brown became involved in the case after being asked to become a plaintiff by attorney Charles Scott, an old childhood friend.

Oliver Brown, 32 at the time the suit against the school district was brought, served as an assistant pastor at Topeka's black Methodist church and as a welder for the Atchison, Topeka, and Santa Fe Railway. A former teacher described Brown as "an average pupil and a good citizen." Shy, hard-working, religious, and clearly no militant, Brown became the non-threatening face of the lawsuit.

Brown and his wife had three children, ages 8, 4, and 5 months at the time of trial. Linda Brown attended all-black Monroe Elementary, a school located 21 blocks from their home on West First Street. Oliver Brown testified that "many times [Linda] had to wait through cold, the rain, and the snow" for a bus to take her to Monroe, even though the family lived only seven blocks from an all-white elementary school. Oliver also testified that Linda's route to her bus stop took her over a "main thoroughfare . . . with a vast amount of traffic."

By the time the Supreme Court announced its decision in *Brown*, and the Topeka schools desegregated, Linda had moved on to a previously integrated junior high school. Linda's siblings, however, enjoyed the benefits of a desegregated elementary school education.

Oliver Brown and his family moved to Springfield, Missouri in 1959 where he served as a minister. He died of a heart attack in 1961.

SOURCE. *Douglas O. Linder, "Meet the Browns: Esther Brown and the Oliver Brown Family," Famous Trials: The* Brown v. Board of Education of Topeka *Trial, University of Missouri-Kansas City (UMKC) School of Law, 2011. http://law2.umkc.edu/faculty/projects/ftrials/brownvboard/meetthebrowns.html.*

be a decision to keep African Americans as near as possible to their former state of slavery. According to Marshall, such a decision would be equivalent to saying that "Negroes are inferior to all other human beings."

South Carolina's Argument

John W. Davis, who was legal counsel for the state of South Carolina, argued in his closing remarks that the state had honored *Plessy*'s separate-but-equal doctrine through large investments in schools for black students. He claimed that the state had the intention of creating a condition of equality for children of all races and that "the happiness, the progress and the welfare of these children is best promoted in segregated schools." He also maintained that it was not within the jurisdiction of the U.S. Supreme Court to decide how the state of South Carolina conducted its school system. He told the Court:

> Your Honors do not sit, and cannot sit as a glorified Board of Education for the State of South Carolina or any other state. . . . Neither this Court nor any other court . . . can sit in the chairs of the legislature of South Carolina and mold its educational system, and if it is found to be in its present form unacceptable, the State of South Carolina must devise the alternative.

On the same day that the Court handed down its decision in *Brown*, it decided the related case of *Bolling*. Applying the same principles that it had used in *Brown*, the Court ruled in *Bolling* that racial segregation of schoolchildren in the District of Columbia was unconstitutional.

Brown II Enforces the Ruling to Desegregate

In the following year, the Supreme Court on reargument made another decision in *Brown* that was designed to establish the methodology by which to enforce deseg-

> *Brown* fostered changes in the legal and moral outlook of the country that greatly aided future efforts to end racial discrimination.

regation of public schools. *Brown II* (1955), as it has come to be called, determined that school authorities had the principal responsibility for evaluating and solving local educational problems, including those resulting from segregation. The Court decided to remand (send back) the individual cases in *Brown* to lower courts in order that those courts might better assess the efforts of school authorities to desegregate the public schools and thereby provide to African American children their equal protection under the laws as promised by the Fourteenth Amendment. The lower courts were directed to take into account any problems concerning school administration, facilities, transportation, and personnel, and to consider any revision of local laws necessary to resolve the problems and achieve desegregation.

Brown v. Board of Education dealt only with government-mandated or government-authorized segregation. It did not apply to racial segregation or discrimination related to restaurants, theaters, employment, country clubs, or other parts of the private sector. However, *Brown* fostered changes in the legal and moral outlook of the country that greatly aided future efforts to end racial discrimination as related to employment, housing, and places of public accommodation, and thus greatly affected U.S. race relations.

The US Supreme Court Codifies "Separate but Equal" into Law

Henry Billings Brown

The following viewpoint is part of the 1896 US Supreme Court decision in *Plessy v. Ferguson*. The decision upholds the legality of racial segregation, which was to remain in effect until the *Brown v. Board of Education* (1954) decision almost sixty years later. *Plessy v. Ferguson* revolved around a law requiring separate train coaches for African Americans in the state of Louisiana. In its decision, the court rules that such "separate but equal" accommodation laws do not violate the Thirteenth Amendment abolishing slavery or the Fourteenth Amendment guaranteeing equal protection to all citizens. The court distinguishes between laws requiring separate accommodations and those interfering with political rights, such as voting. The court concludes that legislation is powerless to stop prejudice and racial antipathies. Henry Billings Brown was an associate justice of the Supreme Court from 1891 to 1906 and was the author of hundreds of legal opinions as a federal judge.

SOURCE. Henry Billings Brown, Opinion, *Plessy v. Ferguson*, US Supreme Court, May 18, 1896.

This case turns upon the constitutionality of an act of the General Assembly of the State of Louisiana, passed in 1890, providing for separate railway carriages for the white and colored races. . . .

The information filed in the criminal District Court charged in substance that Plessy, being a passenger between two stations within the State of Louisiana, was assigned by officers of the company to the coach used for the race to which he belonged, but he insisted upon going into a coach used by the race to which he did not belong. Neither in the information nor plea was his particular race or color averred. The petition for the writ of prohibition averred that petitioner was seven-eighths Caucasian and one eighth African blood; that the mixture of colored blood was not discernible in him, and that he was entitled to every right, privilege and immunity secured to citizens of the United States of the white race; and that, upon such theory, he took possession of a vacant seat in a coach where passengers of the white race were accommodated, and was ordered by the conductor to vacate said coach and take a seat in another assigned to persons of the colored race, and, having refused to comply with such demand, he was forcibly ejected with the aid of a police officer, and imprisoned in the parish jail to answer a charge of having violated the [Louisiana] act.

The constitutionality of this act is attacked upon the ground that it conflicts both with the Thirteenth Amendment of the Constitution, abolishing slavery, and the Fourteenth Amendment, which prohibits certain restrictive legislation on the part of the States.

1. That it does not conflict with the Thirteenth Amendment, which abolished slavery and involuntary servitude, except as a punishment for crime, is too clear for argument. Slavery implies involuntary servitude—a state of bondage; the ownership of mankind as a chattel, or at least the control of the labor and services of

Laws permitting, and even requiring, their separation in places where they are liable to be brought into contact do not necessarily imply the inferiority of either race to the other.

one man for the benefit of another, and the absence of a legal right to the disposal of his own person, property and services. . . .

2. By the Fourteenth Amendment, all persons born or naturalized in the United States and subject to the jurisdiction thereof are made citizens of the United States and of the State wherein they reside, and the States are forbidden from making or enforcing any law which shall abridge the privileges or immunities of citizens of the United States, or shall deprive any person of life, liberty, or property without due process of law, or deny to any person within their jurisdiction the equal protection of the laws. . . .

The History of Laws Allowing Segregation

The object of the amendment was undoubtedly to enforce the absolute equality of the two races before the law, but, in the nature of things, it could not have been intended to abolish distinctions based upon color, or to enforce social, as distinguished from political, equality, or a commingling of the two races upon terms unsatisfactory to either. Laws permitting, and even requiring, their separation in places where they are liable to be brought into contact do not necessarily imply the inferiority of either race to the other, and have been generally, if not universally, recognized as within the competency of the state legislatures in the exercise of their police power. The most common instance of this is connected with the establishment of separate schools for white and colored children, which has been held to be a valid exercise of the legislative power even by courts of States where the political rights of the colored race have been longest and most earnestly enforced.

African American students exercise outside a segregated, one-room school in the late nineteenth century after the *Plessy v. Ferguson* Supreme Court decision. **© Afro American Newspapers/Gado/Getty Images.**

One of the earliest of these cases is that of *Roberts v. City of Boston*, in which the Supreme Judicial Court of Massachusetts held that the general school committee of Boston had power to make provision for the instruction of colored children in separate schools established exclusively for them, and to prohibit their attendance upon the other schools. "The great principle," said Chief Justice Shaw, "advanced by the learned and eloquent advocate for the plaintiff" (Mr. Charles Sumner):

> is that, by the constitution and laws of Massachusetts, all persons without distinction of age or sex, birth or color, origin or condition, are equal before the law. . . . But when this great principle comes to be applied to the actual and various conditions of persons in society, it will not warrant the assertion that men and women are

> legally clothed with the same civil and political powers, and that children and adults are legally to have the same functions and be subject to the same treatment, but only that the rights of all, as they are settled and regulated by law, are equally entitled to the paternal consideration and protection of the law for their maintenance and security.

It was held that the powers of the committee extended to the establishment of separate schools for children of different ages, sexes and colors, and that they might also establish special schools for poor and neglected children, who have become too old to attend the primary school and yet have not acquired the rudiments of learning to enable them to enter the ordinary schools. Similar laws have been enacted by Congress under its general power of legislation over the District of Columbia, as well as by the legislatures of many of the States, and have been generally, if not uniformly, sustained by the courts.

"The distinction between laws interfering with the political equality of the negro and those requiring the separation of the two races . . . has been frequently drawn by this court."

Laws forbidding the intermarriage of the two races may be said in a technical sense to interfere with the freedom of contract, and yet have been universally recognized as within the police power of the State.

The distinction between laws interfering with the political equality of the negro and those requiring the separation of the two races in schools, theatres and railway carriages has been frequently drawn by this court. . . .

Legislation Cannot Prevent Prejudice

So far, then, as a conflict with the Fourteenth Amendment is concerned, the case reduces itself to the ques-

Excerpts from John Harlan's Dissent to *Plessy v. Ferguson*

In respect of civil rights, common to all citizens, the Constitution of the United States does not, I think permit any public authority to know the race of those entitled to be protected in the enjoyment of such rights. Every true man has pride of race, and under appropriate circumstances which the rights of others, his equals before the law, are not to be affected, it is his privilege to express such pride and to take such action based upon it as to him seems proper. But I deny that any legislative body or judicial tribunal may have regard to the race of citizens which the civil rights of those citizens are involved. Indeed, such legislation as that here in question is inconsistent not only with that equality of rights which pertains to citizenship, national and state but with the personal liberty enjoyed by everyone within the United States. . . .

The arbitrary separation of citizens, on the basis of race, while they are on a public highway, is a badge of servitude wholly inconsistent with the civil freedom and the equality before the law established by the Constitution. It cannot be justified upon any legal grounds.

If evils will result from the commingling of the two races upon public highways established for the benefit of all, they will infinitely less than those that will surely come from state legislation regulating the enjoyment of civil rights upon the basis of race. We boast of the freedom enjoyed by our people above all other peoples. But it is difficult to reconcile that boast with the state of the law which, practically, puts the brand of servitude and degradation upon a large class of our fellow citizens, our equals before the law. The thin disguise of "equal" accommodations for passengers in railroad coaches will not mislead anyone, nor atone for the wrong this day done.

SOURCE. *John Marshall Harlan, Dissent,* Plessy v. Ferguson, *US Supreme Court, 1896*

tion whether the statute of Louisiana is a reasonable regulation, and, with respect to this, there must necessarily be a large discretion on the part of the legislature. In determining the question of reasonableness, it is at liberty to act with reference to the established usages, customs, and traditions of the people, and with a view to the promotion of their comfort and the preservation of the public peace and good order. Gauged by this standard, we cannot say that a law which authorizes or even requires the separation of the two races in public conveyances is unreasonable, or more obnoxious to the Fourteenth Amendment than the acts of Congress requiring separate schools for colored children in the District of Columbia, the constitutionality of which does not seem to have been questioned, or the corresponding acts of state legislatures.

We consider the underlying fallacy of the plaintiff's argument to consist in the assumption that the enforced separation of the two races stamps the colored race with a badge of inferiority. If this be so, it is not by reason of anything found in the act, but solely because the colored race chooses to put that construction upon it. The argument necessarily assumes that if, as has been more than once the case and is not unlikely to be so again, the colored race should become the dominant power in the state legislature, and should enact a law in precisely similar terms, it would thereby relegate the white race to an inferior position. We imagine that the white race, at least, would not acquiesce in this assumption. The argument also assumes that social prejudices may be overcome by legislation, and that equal rights cannot be secured to the negro except by an enforced commingling of the two races. We cannot accept this proposition. If the two races are to meet upon terms of social equality, it must be the result of natural affinities, a mutual appreciation of each other's merits, and a voluntary consent of individuals. As was

> "Legislation is powerless to eradicate racial instincts or to abolish distinctions based upon physical differences."

said by the Court of Appeals of New York in *People v. Gallagher*,

> this end can neither be accomplished nor promoted by laws which conflict with the general sentiment of the community upon whom they are designed to operate. When the government, therefore, has secured to each of its citizens equal rights before the law and equal opportunities for improvement and progress, it has accomplished the end for which it was organized, and performed all of the functions respecting social advantages with which it is endowed.

Legislation is powerless to eradicate racial instincts or to abolish distinctions based upon physical differences, and the attempt to do so can only result in accentuating the difficulties of the present situation. If the civil and political rights of both races be equal, one cannot be inferior to the other civilly or politically. If one race be inferior to the other socially, the Constitution of the United States cannot put them upon the same plane.

In Two Landmark Rulings, the US Supreme Court Declares School Segregation Unconstitutional

Earl Warren

In the following viewpoint, the US Supreme Court ends racial segregation in public schools in the 1954 *Brown v. Board of Education* ruling. The decision, known colloquially as *Brown v. Board*, was actually two separate rulings by the court, *Brown I* in 1954 and *Brown II* in 1955. In opinions written by Justice Earl Warren, the Supreme Court first reverses the decades-long precedent of "separate but equal" (in *Brown I*) and then orders states to end segregation with "all deliberate speed" (*Brown II*). The court finds that school segregation laws are in violation of the US Constitution because they deprive citizens of the

---

SOURCE. Earl Warren, Opinions, *Brown v. Board of Education*, US Supreme Court, May 17, 1954 (*Brown I*), and May 31, 1955 (*Brown II*).

equal protection guaranteed by the Fourteenth Amendment. In *Brown II*, Warren writes of the importance of the constitutional principles in the initial decision and orders the removal of any obstacles to the implementation of the court's ruling. Warren was the fourteenth chief justice of the United States, serving from 1953 to 1969.

These cases come to us from the States of Kansas, South Carolina, Virginia, and Delaware. They are premised on different facts and different local conditions, but a common legal question justifies their consideration together in this consolidated opinion.

In each of the cases, minors of the Negro race, through their legal representatives, seek the aid of the courts in obtaining admission to the public schools of their community on a nonsegregated basis. In each instance, they had been denied admission to schools attended by white children under laws requiring or permitting segregation according to race. This segregation was alleged to deprive the plaintiffs of the equal protection of the laws under the Fourteenth Amendment. In each of the cases other than the Delaware case, a three-judge federal district court denied relief to the plaintiffs on the so-called "separate but equal" doctrine announced by this Court in *Plessy v. Ferguson*. Under that doctrine, equality of treatment is accorded when the races are provided substantially equal facilities, even though these facilities be separate. In the Delaware case, the Supreme Court of Delaware adhered to that doctrine, but ordered that the plaintiffs be admitted to the white schools because of their superiority to the Negro schools.

The plaintiffs contend that segregated public schools are not "equal" and cannot be made "equal," and that hence they are deprived of the equal protection of the laws. Because of the obvious importance of the question presented, the Court took jurisdiction. Argument was heard in the 1952 Term, and reargument was heard this Term on certain questions propounded by the Court.

The Fourteenth Amendment and Racial Segregation

Reargument was largely devoted to the circumstances surrounding the adoption of the Fourteenth Amendment in 1868. It covered exhaustively consideration of the Amendment in Congress, ratification by the states, then-existing practices in racial segregation, and the views of proponents and opponents of the Amendment. This discussion and our own investigation convince us that, although these sources cast some light, it is not enough to resolve the problem with which we are faced. At best, they are inconclusive. The most avid proponents of the post-War Amendments undoubtedly intended them to remove all legal distinctions among "all persons born or naturalized in the United States." Their opponents, just as certainly, were antagonistic to both the letter and the spirit of the Amendments and wished them to have the most limited effect. What others in Congress and the state legislatures had in mind cannot be determined with any degree of certainty.

An additional reason for the inconclusive nature of the Amendment's history with respect to segregated schools is the status of public education at that time. In the South, the movement toward free common schools, supported by general taxation, had not yet taken hold. Education of white children was largely in the hands of private groups. Education of Negroes was almost nonexistent, and practically all of the race were illiterate. In fact, any education of Negroes was forbidden by law in some states. Today, in contrast, many Negroes have achieved outstanding success in the arts and sciences, as well as in the business and professional world. It is true that public school education at the time of the Amendment had advanced further in the North, but the effect

SEGREGATION IN US PUBLIC SCHOOLS PRIOR TO *BROWN V. BOARD OF EDUCATION*

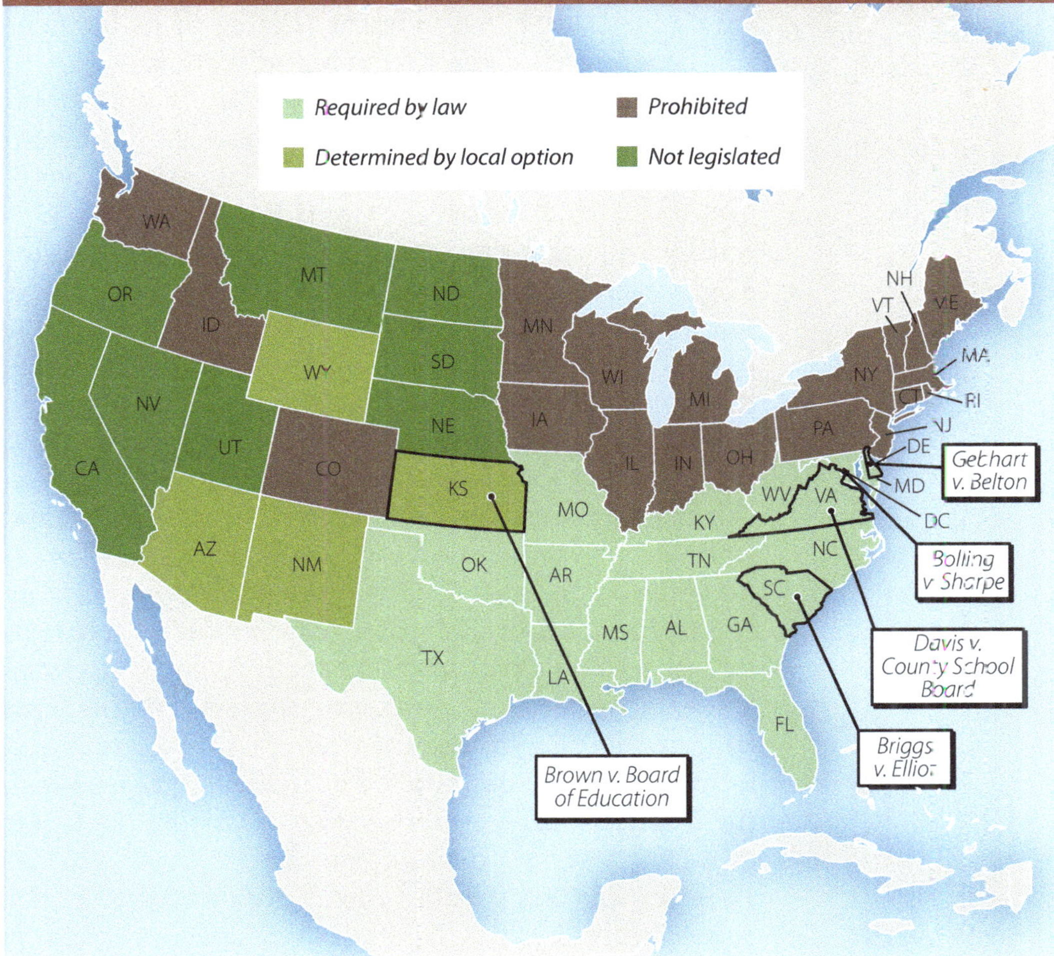

of the Amendment on Northern States was generally ignored in the congressional debates. Even in the North, the conditions of public education did not approximate those existing today. The curriculum was usually rudimentary; ungraded schools were common in rural areas; the school term was but three months a year in many states, and compulsory school attendance was virtually

> It is not surprising that there should be so little in the history of the Fourteenth Amendment relating to its intended effect on public education.

unknown. As a consequence, it is not surprising that there should be so little in the history of the Fourteenth Amendment relating to its intended effect on public education.

In the first cases in this Court construing the Fourteenth Amendment, decided shortly after its adoption, the Court interpreted it as proscribing all state-imposed discriminations against the Negro race. The doctrine of "separate but equal" did not make its appearance in this Court until 1896 in the case of *Plessy v. Ferguson*, involving not education but transportation. American courts have since labored with the doctrine for over half a century. In this Court, there have been six cases involving the "separate but equal" doctrine in the field of public education. In *Cumming v. County Board of Education* and *Gong Lum v. Rice* the validity of the doctrine itself was not challenged. In more recent cases, all on the graduate school level, inequality was found in that specific benefits enjoyed by white students were denied to Negro students of the same educational qualifications. In none of these cases was it necessary to reexamine the doctrine to grant relief to the Negro plaintiff. And in *Sweatt v. Painter*, the Court expressly reserved decision on the question whether *Plessy v. Ferguson* should be held inapplicable to public education.

The Tangible Effects of Segregation

In the instant cases, that question is directly presented. Here, unlike *Sweatt v. Painter*, there are findings below that the Negro and white schools involved have been equalized, or are being equalized, with respect to buildings, curricula, qualifications and salaries of teachers, and other "tangible" factors. Our decision, therefore, cannot turn on merely a comparison of these tangible factors in the Negro and white schools involved in each of the cases. We must look instead to the effect of segregation itself on public education.

> Does segregation of children in public schools solely on the basis of race . . . deprive the children of the minority group of equal education opportunities? We believe that it does.

In approaching this problem, we cannot turn the clock back to 1868, when the Amendment was adopted, or even to 1896, when *Plessy v. Ferguson* was written. We must consider public education in the light of its full development and its present place in American life throughout the Nation. Only in this way can it be determined if segregation in public schools deprives these plaintiffs of the equal protection of the laws.

Today, education is perhaps the most important function of state and local governments. Compulsory school attendance laws and the great expenditures for education both demonstrate our recognition of the importance of education to our democratic society. It is required in the performance of our most basic public responsibilities, even service in the armed forces. It is the very foundation of good citizenship. Today it is a principal instrument in awakening the child to cultural values, in preparing him for later professional training, and in helping him to adjust normally to his environment. In these days, it is doubtful that any child may reasonably be expected to succeed in life if he is denied the opportunity of an education. Such an opportunity, where the state has undertaken to provide it, is a right which must be made available to all on equal terms.

We come then to the question presented: Does segregation of children in public schools solely on the basis of race, even though the physical facilities and other "tangible" factors may be equal, deprive the children of the minority group of equal educational opportunities? We believe that it does.

Intangible Effects of Segregation Harm Children

In *Sweatt v. Painter*, supra, in finding that a segregated law school for Negroes could not provide them equal educational opportunities, this Court relied in large part on "those qualities which are incapable of objective measurement but which make for greatness in a law school." In *McLaurin v. Oklahoma State Regents*, the Court, in requiring that a Negro admitted to a white graduate school be treated like all other students, again resorted to intangible considerations: ". . . his ability to study, to engage

US Supreme Court Chief Justice Earl Warren wrote the decision on the landmark case of *Brown v. Board of Education*, which ended the "separate but equal" doctrine and desegregated schools. **© Bachrach/ Getty Images.**

in discussions and exchange views with other students, and, in general, to learn his profession." Such considerations apply with added force to children in grade and high schools. To separate them from others of similar age and qualifications solely because of their race generates a feeling of inferiority as to their status in the community that may affect their hearts and minds in a way unlikely ever to be undone. The effect of this separation on their educational opportunities was well stated by a finding in the Kansas case by a court which nevertheless felt compelled to rule against the Negro plaintiffs:

Segregation of white and colored children in public schools has a detrimental effect upon the colored children. The impact is greater when it has the sanction of the law, for the policy of separating the races is usually interpreted as denoting the inferiority of the negro group. A sense of inferiority affects the motivation of a child to learn. Segregation with the sanction of law, therefore, has a tendency to [retard] the educational and mental development of negro children and to deprive them of some of the benefits they would receive in a racial[ly] integrated school system.

> Separate educational facilities are inherently unequal.

Whatever may have been the extent of psychological knowledge at the time of *Plessy v. Ferguson*, this finding is amply supported by modern authority. Any language in *Plessy v. Ferguson* contrary to this finding is rejected.

Separate Facilities Violate the Constitution

We conclude that, in the field of public education, the doctrine of "separate but equal" has no place. Separate educational facilities are inherently unequal. Therefore, we hold that the plaintiffs and others similarly situated for whom the actions have been brought are, by reason of the segregation complained of, deprived of the equal protection of the laws guaranteed by the Fourteenth Amendment. This disposition makes unnecessary any discussion whether such segregation also violates the Due Process Clause of the Fourteenth Amendment.

Because these are class actions, because of the wide applicability of this decision, and because of the great variety of local conditions, the formulation of decrees in these cases presents problems of considerable complexity. On reargument, the consideration of appropriate relief was necessarily subordinated to the primary question—the constitutionality of segregation in public education. We have now announced that such segregation is a denial of the equal protection of the laws. In order that we may have the full assistance of the parties in formulating decrees, the cases will be restored to the docket, and the parties are requested to present further argument on Questions 4 and 5 previously propounded by the Court for the reargument this Term The Attorney General of the United States is again invited to participate. The Attorneys General of the states requiring or permitting segregation in public education will also be permitted to appear as amici curiae upon request to do so by September 15, 1954, and submission of briefs by October 1, 1954.

It is so ordered.

The *Brown II* Decision, 1955

The opinions [May 17, 1954], declaring the fundamental principle that racial discrimination in public education is unconstitutional, are incorporated herein by reference. All provisions of federal, state, or local law requiring or permitting such discrimination must yield to this principle. There remains for consideration the manner in which relief is to be accorded.

Because these cases arose under different local conditions and their disposition will involve a variety of local problems, we requested further argument on the question of relief. In view of the nationwide importance of the decision, we invited the Attorney General of the United States and the Attorneys General of all states requiring or permitting racial discrimination in public education to present their views on that question. The parties, the United States, and the States of Florida, North Carolina, Arkansas, Oklahoma, Maryland, and Texas filed briefs and participated in the oral argument.

These presentations were informative and helpful to the Court in its consideration of the complexities arising from the transition to a system of public education freed of racial discrimination. The presentations also demonstrated that substantial steps to eliminate racial discrimination in public schools have already been taken, not only in some of the communities in which these cases arose, but in some of the states appearing as amici curiae, and in other states as well. Substantial progress has been made in the District of Columbia and in the communities in Kansas and Delaware involved in this litigation. The defendants in the cases coming to us from South Carolina and Virginia are awaiting the decision of this Court concerning relief.

Implementation Remanded to Lower Courts

Full implementation of these constitutional principles may require solution of varied local school problems. School authorities have the primary responsibility for elucidating, assessing, and solving these problems; courts will have to consider whether the action of school authorities constitutes good faith implementation of the governing constitutional principles. Because of their proximity to local conditions and the possible need for further hearings, the courts which originally heard these cases can best perform this judicial appraisal. Accordingly, we believe it appropriate to remand the cases to those courts.

> The vitality of these constitutional principles cannot be allowed to yield simply because of disagreement with them.

In fashioning and effectuating the decrees, the courts will be guided by equitable principles. Traditionally, equity has been characterized by a practical flexibility in shaping its remedies and by a facility for adjusting and reconciling public and private needs. These cases call for the exercise of these traditional attributes of equity power. At stake is the personal interest of the plaintiffs in admission to public schools as soon as practicable on a nondiscriminatory basis. To effectuate this interest may call for elimination of a variety of obstacles in making the transition to school systems operated in accordance with the constitutional principles set forth in our May 17, 1954, decision. Courts of equity may properly take into account the public interest in the elimination of such obstacles in a systematic and effective manner. But it should go without saying that **the vitality of these constitutional principles cannot be allowed to yield simply because of disagreement with them.**

While giving weight to these public and private considerations, the courts will require that the defendants make a prompt and reasonable start toward full compliance with our May 17, 1954, ruling. Once such a start has been made, the courts may find that additional time is necessary to carry out the ruling in an effective manner. The burden rests upon the defendants to establish that such time is necessary in the public interest and is consistent with good faith compliance at the earliest practicable date. To that end, the courts may consider problems related to administration, arising from the physical condition of the school plant, the school transportation system, personnel, revision of school districts and attendance areas into compact units to achieve a system of determining admission to the public schools on a nonracial basis, and revision of local laws and regulations which may be necessary in solving the foregoing problems. They will also consider the adequacy of any plans the defendants may propose to meet these problems and to effectuate a transition to a racially nondiscriminatory school system. During this period of transition, the courts will retain jurisdiction of these cases.

Integration Must Proceed with Deliberate Speed

The judgments below, except that, in the Delaware case, are accordingly reversed, and the cases are remanded to the District Courts to take such proceedings and enter such orders and decrees consistent with this opinion as are necessary and proper to admit to public schools on a racially nondiscriminatory basis with all deliberate speed the parties to these cases. The judgment in the Delaware case—ordering the immediate admission of the plaintiffs to schools previously attended only by white children—is affirmed on the basis of the principles stated in our May 17, 1954, opinion, but the case is remanded to the Supreme Court of Delaware for such further proceedings as that Court may deem necessary in light of this opinion.

It is so ordered.

VIEWPOINT 4

Southern Legislators Vow to Oppose Desegregation

Members of the US Congress

The following viewpoint was signed by ninety-nine members of Congress in 1956 in protest of the recent US Supreme Court decision in *Brown v. Board of Education* (1954). The document is called the "The Declaration of Constitutional Principles" and is commonly known as the "Southern Manifesto" because the nineteen senators and eighty-two representatives who signed it were from the South. In the document, the congressmen decry what they feel is an abuse of judicial power and an encroachment of states' rights. The authors also explain that "separate but equal" principles had been previously upheld by the courts as not violating the Fourteenth Amendment, and the practice is part of life in their home states. They commend those who vow to resist forced integration and ask states not directly affected by the decision to also resist judicial encroachment.

SOURCE. "Southern Manifesto on Integration (March 12, 1956)," *Congressional Record, 84th Congress Second Session*, vol. 102, part 4. Washington, DC: Governmental Printing Office, 1956, pp. 4459–4460.

The unwarranted decision of the Supreme Court in the public school cases is now bearing the fruit always produced when men substitute naked power for established law.

The Founding Fathers gave us a Constitution of checks and balances because they realized the inescapable lesson of history that no man or group of men can be safely entrusted with unlimited power. They framed this Constitution with its provisions for change by amendment in order to secure the fundamentals of government against the dangers of temporary popular passion or the personal predilections of public officeholders.

"The original Constitutional does not mention education. Neither does the Fourteenth Amendment nor any other amendment."

We regard the decision of the Supreme Court in the school cases as clear abuse of judicial power. It climaxes a trend in the Federal judiciary undertaking to legislate, in derogation of the authority of Congress, and to encroach upon the reserved rights of the states and the people.

The Fourteenth Amendment Does Not Apply to Education

The original Constitutional does not mention education. Neither does the Fourteenth Amendment nor any other amendment. The debates preceding the submission of the Fourteenth Amendment clearly show that there was no intent that it should affect the systems of education maintained by the states.

The very Congress which proposed the amendment subsequently provided for segregated schools in the District of Columbia.

When the amendment was adopted in 1868, there were thirty-seven states of the Union. Every one of the twenty-six states that had any substantial racial differences among its people either approved the operation

The NAACP's Atlanta Declaration

We, as representatives of the NAACP from 17 Southern and Border States and the District of Columbia, have assembled here, May 22–23, for the purpose of collectively developing a program to meet the vital and urgent issues arising out of the historic United States Supreme Court decision of May 17, banning segregation in public schools.

All Americans are now relieved to have the law of the land declare in the clearest language: ". . . in the field of public education the doctrine of 'separate but equal' has no place. Separate educational facilities are inherently unequal." Segregation in public education is now not only unlawful; it is un-American. True Americans are grateful for this decision. Now that the law is made clear, we look to the future. Having canvassed the situation in each of our states, we approach the future with the utmost confidence. This confidence is based upon many factors including the pledges of support and compliance by governors, attorneys general, mayors and education officials; and by enlightened guidance of newspaper, radio, television and other organs of public communication and comment.

We stand ready to work with other law abiding citizens who are anxious to translate this decision into a program of action to eradicate racial segregation in public education as speedily as possible.

We are instructing all of our branches in every affected area to petition their local school boards to abolish segregation without delay and to assist

of segregated schools already in existence or subsequently established such schools by action of the same law-making body which considered the Fourteenth Amendment.

As admitted by the Supreme Court in the public school case (*Brown v. Board of Education*), the doctrine of separate but equal schools "apparently originated in *Roberts v. City of Boston* (1849), upholding school segregation against attack as being violative of a state constitutional guarantee of equality." This constitutional doctrine began in the North—not in the South—and it these agencies in working out ways and means of implementing the Court's ruling. The total resources of the NAACP will be made available to facilitate this great project of ending the artificial separation of America's children on the irrelevant basis of race and color.

While we recognize that school officials will have certain administrative problems in transferring from a segregated to a nonsegregated system, we will resist the use of any tactics contrived for the sole purpose of delaying desegregation.

In pursuit of our objectives, we will accelerate our community action program to win public acceptance of the Court's desegregation order from all segments of the population. . . .

We insist that there should be integration at all levels, including the assignment of teacher-personnel on a non-discriminatory basis. . . .

We look upon this memorable decision not as a victory for Negroes alone, but for the whole American people and as a vindication of America's leadership of the free world.

Lest there be any misunderstanding of our position, we here rededicate ourselves to the removal of all racial segregation in public education and reiterate our determination to achieve this goal without compromise of principle.

SOURCE. *Colin A. Palmer, ed., "The Atlanta Declaration (National Association for the Advancement of Colored People, 1854),"* Encyclopedia of African-American Culture and History, *second edition, vol. 6. Detroit: Macmillan Reference USA, 2006.*

was followed not only in Massachusetts but in Connecticut, New York, Illinois, Indiana, Michigan, Minnesota, New Jersey, Ohio, Pennsylvania and other northern states until they, exercising their rights as states through the constitutional processes of local self-government, changed their school systems.

Segregation Conforms to Established Principles

In the case of *Plessy v. Ferguson* in 1896 the Supreme Court expressly declared that under the Fourteenth Amendment

> The 'separate but equal' principle . . . became a part of the life of the people of many of the states and confirmed their habits, customs, traditions and way of life.

no person was denied any of his rights if the states provided separate but equal public facilities. This decision has been followed in many other cases. It is notable that the Supreme Court, speaking through Chief Justice Taft, a former President of the United States, unanimously declared in 1927 in *Lum v. Rice* that the "separate but equal" principle is "within the discretion of the state in regulating its public schools and does not conflict with the Fourteenth Amendment."

This interpretation, restated time and again, **became a part of the life of the people of many of the states and confirmed their habits, customs, traditions and way of life.** It is founded on elemental humanity and common sense, for parents should not be deprived by Government of the right to direct the lives and education of their own children.

The Court's Decision Has No Legal Basis

Though there has been no constitutional amendment or act of Congress changing this established legal principle almost a century old, the Supreme Court of the United States, with no legal basis for such action, undertook to exercise their naked judicial power and substituted their personal political and social ideas for the established law of the land.

This unwarranted exercise of power by the court, contrary to the Constitution, is creating chaos and confusion in the states principally affected. It is destroying the amicable relations between the white and Negro races that have been created through ninety years of patient effort by the good people of both races. It has planted hatred and suspicion where there has been heretofore friendship and understanding.

Without regard to the consent of the governed, outside agitators are threatening immediate and revolutionary changes in our public school systems. If done, this is certain to destroy the system of public education in some of the states.

With the gravest concern for the explosive and dangerous condition created by this decision and inflamed by outside meddlers.

A Pledge to Peacefully and Lawfully Defy the Court

We reaffirm our reliance on the Constitution as the fundamental law of the land.

We decry the Supreme Court's encroachments on rights reserved to the states and to the people, contrary to established law and to the Constitution.

We commend the motives of those states which have declared the intention to resist forced integration by any lawful means.

A 1963 highway billboard in Alabama expresses the feelings of many Southern legislators and constituents about the *Brown v. Board of Education* decision. It calls for the ouster of the US Supreme Court justice who wrote the opinion, which they criticized as being extraconstitutional. © AP Photo.

We appeal to the states and people who are not directly affected by these decisions to consider the constitutional principles involved against the time when they too, on issues vital to them, may be the victims of judicial encroachment.

Even though we constitute a minority in the present congress, we have full faith that a majority of the American people believe in the dual system of government which has enabled us to achieve our greatness and will in time demand that the reserved rights of the states and of the people be made secure against judicial usurpation.

We pledge ourselves to use all lawful means to bring about a reversal of this decision which is contrary to the Constitution and to prevent the use of force in its implementation.

In this trying period, as we all seek to right this wrong, we appeal to our people not to be provoked by the agitators and troublemakers invading our states and to scrupulously refrain from disorder and lawless acts.

VIEWPOINT 5

Brown Ends the "Shame of Segregation"

Max Freedman

In the following viewpoint, a British journalist reviews the history and implications of the 1954 *Brown v. Board of Education* US Supreme Court decision. He explains that legal segregation can be traced back to Reconstruction, after which African Americans in the South were left without full citizenship rights. The fight for integration, he writes, began in the 1930s with legal cases related to university admission. However it wasn't until *Brown* reached the Supreme Court that the United States was able to strip legal sanction from segregationist policies. This great victory, he says, ends the shame and illegality of segregation in schools, although the end result for African Americans is unknown. Max Freedman was a writer for the *Manchester Guardian*.

The decision of the Supreme Court of the United States that segregation in the public schools is unconstitutional has ended a legal battle of sev-

SOURCE. Max Freedman, "The American Advance," *The Guardian*. May 25, 1954.

Three African American students register at the previously all-white University of South Carolina in 1963, as schools all across the South slowly integrated. © **Rolls Press/ Popperfoto/Getty Images.**

eral generations. Sometimes the contest was marked by stubborn passion; at other periods there was an interlude of lethargy; but the central issues of freedom and equality never were suffered entirely to disappear. It may be instructive to recall the landmarks of this constitutional struggle. For there is a danger that the significance of the Court's verdict may be stained and obscured by an endless haggle over the precise date on which segregation will disappear.

This controversy is rooted in memories of the Civil War, with its incongruous mixture of horrid passion and high-pitched ideals. In 1875 Congress, after a series of sprawling debates passed the Civil Rights Act, which was intended to fulfil the personal rights of every American citizen, regardless of race or colour, as proclaimed in the Fourteenth Amendment. But the act was silent on the subject of schools. In that discordant era the system of public education made small claim on the public conscience or the public purse. Exhausted by war and scarred by the tragedies of the Reconstruction period, the energies of the North recoiled from the task of enforcing the rights of the Negro, won at so tragic a cost. Soon the Negro was left with the shell of citizenship; he was forced into separate schools; and quite often, in the poorer districts, there was no school at all, for white or black. Kentucky was the only Southern state which had compulsory education by 1900. Nearly half the Negro population was unable to read or write. About 85 per cent of the Negro pupils in the South, as recently as 1920, never went beyond the fourth grade. Fewer than 20,000 coloured students attended high school in 1916 throughout the South.

A New Social Conscience

In 1896 the Supreme Court had before it a case brought by a Negro, Plessy by name, who protested against being compelled by a Louisiana statute to sit apart from white passengers on trains in that state. The Court in its majority decision upheld compulsory segregation; and in one of those random generalisations which have stirred so many needless quarrels in the history of jurisprudence it went beyond the point at issue and asserted the power of states to enforce "separate schools for white and coloured children." In this casual and indirect fashion did the doctrine of "separate but equal rights," later to be the theme of strenuous debate, first appear in national affairs. The reality was much harsher than the doctrine, for the Negro endured separation without knowing equality. Between 1896 and 1930 the Supreme Court dealt with problems of Negro education only three times. It never upset or weakened the doctrine established by the *Plessy v. Ferguson* decision.

Then came the sudden flowering of the liberal spirit when Franklin Roosevelt became the nation's leader and out of an unprecedented crisis sent the New Deal to challenge ancient evil and social weakness. The commotion of the great experiment had unfortunate results as well as happy achievements. But it changed almost everything it touched; and among the groups which responded to the new impulses in Washington few showed greater zeal than the leaders of the Negro race, now banded into protective association on a national scale, with ample budgets and dedicated ideals to sustain their cause. Cries of Negro arrogance formed the rasping refrain of critics who resented this surge towards equality; others saw in the very fierceness of this campaign the delayed retribution for the long years of neglect and injustice. At all events the Negro leaders decided to attack segregation in education and to make the Supreme Court the forum of their battle.

Members of the Supreme Court [were] under the vigilant scrutiny of world opinion and amid the restraint of new social concepts astir in the United States.

They were influenced in this decision by at least three different causes. They knew that the mind of the South no longer responded to the old squalid watchwords of hate and violence. Many evils still distorted the image of American freedom, but the South was moving away from the harsh inheritance which stained its gracious civilisation; and in its new temper it would honour the mandate of the American conscience even though the Negro gained rights long thought to be beyond his reach. Secondly, they believed that the principle of segregation could be successfully assailed on legal grounds as a violation of the rights guaranteed by the American Constitution. Finally, they were confident that it would be very hard for members of the Supreme Court, under the vigilant scrutiny of world opinion and amid the restraint of new social concepts astir in the

United States, to pledge their allegiance to the continued enforcement of racial discrimination.

Schools as Racial Battlegrounds

Anyway, the Negroes resolved to test the issue. They decided to raise as least inflammatory the question of the complete exclusion of the Negro from graduate and professional schools operated by the State or his compulsory segregation under conditions of inferiority even if he were admitted to a State University. The first case came before the Supreme Court in 1935, and over the years, especially from 1948 to 1950, the Court handed down decisions which struck at discrimination. Quite often the Court ruled that the treatment of the Negro was not really equal even under the Plessy doctrine, but until the present cases it never held that segregation, in and by itself, was "inherently unequal" and therefore unconstitutional. By 1953 only five state universities in the South still refused to admit Negro students.

It would be wrong, however, to assume that the Negroes rushed to fill the universities. Many Negroes still lack the necessary training for university life. Some who have the requisite ability prefer the coloured colleges in the Northern states or the Northern universities which freely admit Negroes. Yet there is often a quiet form of communal pressure among Negro leaders to select the best students for enrolment at these Southern colleges during this initial period of experiment. Protestant and Catholic universities, of their own choice, have accepted the Court's decision and admitted Negro students, even though many lawyers believe that the Court's judgments are binding only upon colleges run by the State.

Physical violence has stained no campus. Negro students have entered freely into the academic life of the various universities, but their record has by no means always been very distinguished. Almost without exception they do not live in mixed residences, bathe in the same

> When the public school cases were argued before the Court, the American people suddenly realised that the final stage of the constitutional struggle had at last been reached.

pool with white students, or share the exuberant social life which forms the general pattern outside the classroom. In short, the disappearance of segregation by no means implies that the Negroes' problems have been solved even in the favoured atmosphere of the university.

When the public school cases were argued before the Court the American people suddenly realised that the final stage of the constitutional struggle had at least been reached. The real Citadel of privilege was under attack. Here was no small minority of trained students seeking admission to courses of advanced study. More than two million Negro children claim the right to sit in absolute equality in the same classroom with white children. The case went forward while a few Southern states threatened reprisals and vowed to abolish the public school system rather than accept the end of segregation. A solemn passion thrilled through the arguments of the Negro lawyers, led by Mr Thurgood Marshall, as they urged the Court to take a giant stride towards admitting the Negro to the full family of American citizenship—at least in constitutional principle—by outlawing segregation in elementary and high schools. The Court, after two years of argument and after months of deliberation, responded to that plea. By a creative exercise of judicial statesmanship it was able to resolve all its discord and to speak with one voice through the judgement read by Chief Justice Warren.

Unanimity Ends the Nation's Shame

This unanimity has in itself had a profound influence upon the country. It has subdued many extremists to a mere whimper of protest and given massive reinforcement to the counsels of moderation. The Court also gained credit for caution, and for refusing to bludgeon

Thurgood Marshall

The grandson of a slave, Thurgood Marshall was born in Baltimore, Maryland, in 1908. In 1930 he was denied admission to the University of Maryland Law School because he was black, and the experience had a lasting effect on Marshall's personal and professional life. He enrolled at Howard University Law School, and the school's dean, Charles Hamilton, became his mentor. Marshall won his first major court case in 1933 with Hamilton, when they successfully argued against the University of Maryland's racial segregation policies. Marshall also achieved one of Hamilton's chief legal objectives: to overturn the legal basis for "separate but equal" as set forth by *Plessy v. Ferguson* in 1898.

After becoming chief counsel for the National Association for the Advancement of Colored People (NAACP), Marshall amassed an impressive record of Supreme Court challenges to state-sponsored discrimination, including *Brown v. Board of Education* in 1954. President John F. Kennedy appointed Marshall to the US Court of Appeals for the Second Circuit in 1961, and President Lyndon Johnson appointed him US Solicitor General in 1965. Before joining the US Supreme Court in 1967, he had won the majority of the cases he had argued at the Supreme Court. Marshall was the first African American to serve on the Supreme Court or the US Court of Appeals.

According to *Notable Black American Men*, "In a career that spanned 58 years, Marshall achieved an enormous amount. His legal work in the civil rights movement demolished the intellectual and legal basis for the system of racial segregation. His work helped to establish a new standard of racial equality and equal opportunity. In his long career Marshall evolved from civil rights lawyer to civil rights leader to national figure as a US Supreme Court justice."

the South into hasty and provocative action, by wisely deciding to hear additional argument in October on the methods of transition to be followed in establishing the non-segregated school system. Finally, as significant as the gallant restraint of most responsible leaders of Southern opinion is the exemplary caution of the Negroes themselves. They have won a great victory, but they are walking quietly in their hour of exultation. They know they can summon any hostile or recalcitrant Southern state to the bar of the Supreme Court for inevitable judgement; but they are issuing no threats nor proclaiming any manifestos of defiance. It will take many years before the full harvest of the Court's decision can be gathered, but a brave beginning has been made in wisdom, in courage, and in moderation.

In the fundamental area of public education the shame of segregation no longer bears any legal sanction. **The compulsion, pitiless and scorching, that drove the Negro in the South to be treated as the member of an inferior race, and to start this lesson in subjection while still a child, has received the most challenging rebuke** in American history. The Negro may not force his way into white schools; he may rest content with greatly improved coloured schools, now that he has been granted genuine freedom of choice. Governor Byrnes of North Carolina is developing a programme of school construction costing $176 millions, of which $84 millions has been spent since 1951, and 70 per cent of this amount went to build Negro schools. That may well be the guide to the future. By a constructive and cleansing irony never intended, the latest decision of the Supreme Court may result in purging the *Plessy* doctrine of its evil racial taint. It may establish Negro schools that are separate by voluntary choice yet absolutely equal in status and function.

That is one road of advance. The other, less likely, is for Negroes to seek admission in large numbers to the white public schools all over the South, regardless of local irritation or regional custom. Friction there may be, though far less than anyone would have foretold years ago; but after the Court's decision there can be no general retreat into the compulsory shame and illegality of segregation in the schools.

CHAPTER 2

Controversies Surrounding the *Brown v. Board of Education* Trial

VIEWPOINT 1

Court Order Can't Make the Races Mix

Zora Neale Hurston

Photo on previous page: An African American girl eats lunch at her newly-integrated school in the late 1950s. The *Brown* decision had a great effect on many social and cultural issues.

In the following viewpoint, an African American writer explains her reasons for not supporting the US Supreme Court decision to integrate schools. She list several reasons for her disagreement, including having enough pride to not need to associate with those who do not want to associate with African Americans, as well as the belief that segregated schools can provide a quality education. Moreover Hurston writes that the court's order is tantamount to government by decree. She sees ominous similarities to Communist tactics, both in the court's attitude toward African Americans and in what she believes to be an extraconstitutional precedent. Zora Neale Hurston is the author of a number of novels and many short stories, plays, and essays; an anthropological researcher; and an educator. Her best-known novel is *Their Eyes Were Watching God*. She died in 1960.

SOURCE. Zora Neale Hurston, "Letter to the Editor," *Orlando Sentinel*, August 1955. Reproduced by permission.

Editor: I promised God and some other responsible characters, including a bench of bishops that I was not going to part my lips concerning the U.S. Supreme Court decision on ending segregation in public schools of the South. But since a lot of time has passed and no one seems to touch on what to me appears to be the most important point in the hassle, I break my silence just this once. Consider me as just thinking out loud.

The whole matter revolves around the self-respect of my people. How much satisfaction can I get from a court order for somebody to associate with me who does not wish me near them? The American Indian has never been spoken of as a minority and chiefly because there is no whine in the Indian. Certainly he fought, and valiantly for his lands, and rightfully so, but it is inconceivable of an Indian to seek forcible association with anyone. His well-known pride and self-respect would save him from that. I take the Indian position. Now a great clamor will arise in certain quarters that I seek to deny the Negro children of the South their rights, and therefore I am one of those "handkerchief-head niggers" who bow low before the white man and sell out my own people out of cowardice. However an analytical glance will show that that is not the case.

> There has been current the belief that there is no greater delight to Negroes than the physical association with whites.

If there are not adequate Negro schools in Florida, and there is some residual, some inherent and unchangeable quality in white schools, impossible to duplicate anywhere else, then I am the first to insist that Negro Children of Florida be allowed to share this boon. But if there are adequate Negro schools and prepared instructors and instruction, then there is nothing different except the presence of white people.

For this reason, I regard the ruling of the U.S. Supreme Court as insulting rather than honoring my race. Since the days of the never-to-be-sufficiently deplored Reconstruction, **there has been current the belief that there is no greater delight to Negroes than the physical association with whites.** The doctrine of the white mare. Those familiar with the habits of mules are aware that any mule, if not restrained, will automatically follow a white mare. Dishonest mule-traders made money out of this knowledge in the old days.

Lead a white mare along a country road and slyly open the gate and the mules in the lot would run out and follow this mare. This ruling being conceived and brought forth in a sly political medium with eyes on '56, and brought forth in same spirit and for the same purpose, it is clear that they have taken the old notion to heart and acted upon it. It is cunning opening of the barnyard gate with the white mare ambling past. We are expected to hasten pell-mell after her.

It is most astonishing that this should be tried just when the nation is exerting itself to shake off the evils of Communist penetration. It is to be recalled that Moscow, being made aware of this folk belief, made it the main plank in their campaign to win the American Negro from the 1920s on. It was the come-on stuff. Join the party and get yourself a white wife or husband. To supply the expected demand, the party had scraped up this-and-that off of park benches and skid rows were held to be just panting to get hold of one of these objects. Seeing how flat that program fell, it is astonishing that it would be so soon revived. Politics does indeed make strange bedfellows.

But the South had better beware in another direction. While it is being frantic over the segregation ruling, it better keep its eyes open for more important things. One instance of Govt by fiat has been rammed down its throat. It is possible that the end of segregation is not

Photo on following page: American woman of letters Zora Neale Hurston strongly disagreed with the US Supreme Court decision dictating school integration. © **Everett Collection Inc / Alamy.**

here and never meant to be here at present, but the attention of the South directed on what was calculated to keep us busy while more ominous things were brought to pass. The stubborn South and the Midwest kept this nation from being dragged farther to the left than it was during the New Deal.

> A precedent has been established. Government by fiat can replace the constitution.

But what if it is contemplated to do away with the two party system and arrive at Govt by administrative decree? No questions allowed and no information given out from the administrative dept. We could get more rulings on the same subject and more far-reaching any day. It pays to weight every saying and action, however trivial as indicating a trend.

In the ruling on segregation, the unsuspecting nation might have witnessed a trial-balloon. A relatively safe one, since it is sectional and on a matter not likely to arouse other sections of the nation to support of the South. If it goes off fairly well, **a precedent has been established. Govt by fiat can replace the constitution.** You don't have to credit me with too much intelligence and penetration, just so you watch carefully and think.

Meanwhile, personally, I am not delighted. I am not persuaded and elevated by the white mare technique. Negro schools in the state are in very good shape and on the improve. We are fortunate in having Dr. D. E. Williams as head and driving force of Negro instruction. Dr. Williams is relentless in his drive to improve both physical equipment and teacher-quality. He has accomplished wonders in the 20 years past and it is to be expected that he will double that in the future.

It is well known that I have no sympathy nor respect for the "Tragedy of color" school of thought among us, whose fountain-head is the pressure group concerned in this court ruling. I can see no tragedy in being too dark to be invited to a white school social affair. The Supreme Court would have pleased me more if they had concerned themselves about enforcing the compulsory education provisions for Negroes in the South as is done for white children. The next 10 years would be spent in appointing truant officers and looking after conditions in the home from which the children come. Use to the limit what we already have.

> It is a contradiction in terms to scream race pride and equality while at the same time spurning Negro teachers and self-association.

Thems my sentiments and I am sticking by them. Growth from within. Ethical and cultural desegregation. **It is a contradiction in terms to scream race pride and equality while at the same time spurning Negro teachers and self association.** That old white mare business can go racking down the road for all I care.

VIEWPOINT 2

Despite Disappointments, *Brown* Improved African Americans' Lives

David Garrow

In the following viewpoint, a historian reacts to negative appraisals of *Brown v. Board of Education* (1954) on its fiftieth anniversary. He writes that current critiques of the effects of the *Brown* decision attempt to revise, or at least misinterpret, history. In the author's analysis, the *Brown* decision began a series of important reforms that contributed greatly to the African American struggle for freedom. He argues that the problem of continuing segregation is complex and requires a nuanced approach, even though he agrees that some legal arguments for integration hinge on theories of black inferiority. Although there is still work to be done to improve community diversity, the author believes the *Brown* ruling advanced human liberty and should be celebrated as a token of how social reform can be attained through constitutional litigation. David Garrow is the author of *Bearing the Cross*, a Pulitzer–prize winning biography

---

SOURCE. David Garrow, "Give *Brown v. Board of Education* Its Due," *Human Rights Magazine*, vol. 31, no. 3. American Bar Association, Summer 2004. Reproduced by permission.

of Martin Luther King Jr. He writes frequently about the US Supreme Court and the history of civil rights and is currently a research professor of history and law at the University of Pittsburgh School of Law.

This year's fiftieth anniversary of *Brown v. Board of Education* ought to occasion untold praise for the courageous plaintiffs, attorneys, and jurists who helped bring about a momentous reformation of American law. Instead, anniversary celebrations and symposia have been rife with declarations that deprecate, disparage, dismiss, and otherwise dump on *Brown*.

Starting in the 1930s, Thurgood Marshall and the National Association for the Advancement of Colored People (NAACP) Legal Defense Fund litigated a succession of carefully chosen cases for well over a decade in gradually building toward a direct attack on public school segregation. Relying upon local African American communities in four different states—Delaware, Kansas, South Carolina, and Virginia—the NAACP then employed a multifront assault that presented the U.S. Supreme Court with multiple trial records that richly indicted the fundamental inequalities of segregated education.

When the NAACP's first two cases, from South Carolina and Virginia, first reached the Court in 1952, a majority of the nine justices were reluctant to reach any immediate decision. The NAACP's attack challenged not only segregated schools, but also a Court whose own previous Fourteenth Amendment rulings repeatedly had endorsed state-imposed racial separation. Only when the *Brown* cases were reargued for a second time in late 1953 did the nine jurists, led by the newly arrived Chief Justice Earl Warren, slowly move toward a unanimous decision to forcefully reject America's long heritage of legally sanctioned racism.

Current Critiques of *Brown*

When *Brown* was announced on May 17, 1954, supporters and opponents alike greeted it as a landmark moment in American history. Local activists drew inspiration and encouragement from the ruling. Yet many present appraisals of *Brown* differ almost completely from contemporaneous reactions. Today, prominent African Americans have branded *Brown* a failure. New York University law professor Derrick Bell, a former civil rights attorney, offers a depressingly negative treatment of *Brown*'s promise in his latest book, *Silent Covenants*, as does Harvard law professor Charles Ogletree in *All Deliberate Speed*. In addition, academics such as Gerald Rosenberg of the University of Chicago, in *The Hollow Hope*, and Michael Klarman of the University of Virginia, in *From Jim Crow to Civil Rights*, contend that *Brown* did little to advance the African American freedom struggle.

Many present appraisals of *Brown* differ almost completely from contemporaneous reactions. Today, prominent African Americans have branded *Brown* a failure.

Current African American and liberal critiques of *Brown* feature two predominant themes. One is the familiar statement that public schools in America's largest cities, but also in suburbs both northern and southern, remain highly segregated by race notwithstanding *Brown*'s constitutional fame. The other, which stands in some tension with the first, is that the current African American ambivalence about school integration, so visible in most black communities nowadays, is preferable to the naïve belief in integration that civil rights leaders articulated in the initial decade after the *Brown* decision.

The first complaint revisits well-trod historical ground. With the almost singular exception of the 1958 Little Rock school case, *Cooper v. Aaron*, the Supreme Court did indeed pursue a largely hands-off approach to desegregation of southern schools until 1968. Then,

US COLLEGE ENROLLMENT OF BLACK AND WHITE STUDENTS, 1967–2010

Enrollment in degree-granting institutions as a percent of all 18- to 24-year-olds by race/ethnicity of student, 1967 through 2010.

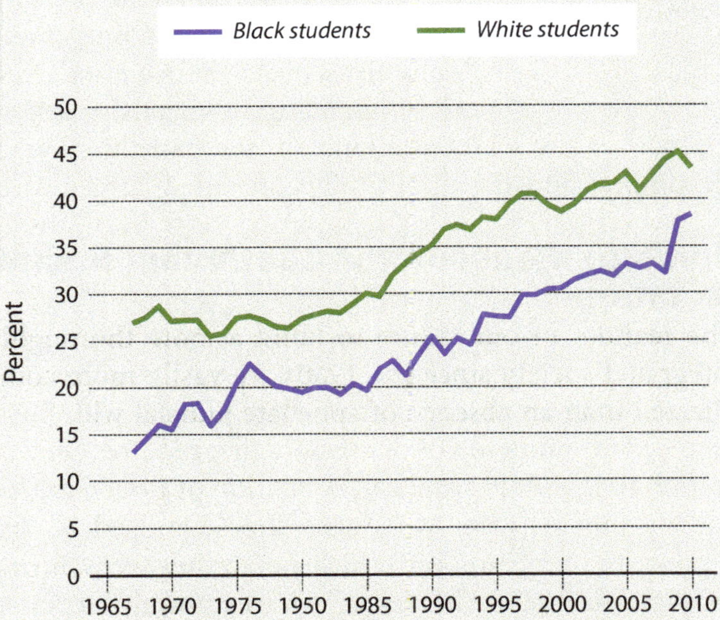

Taken from: National Center for Education Statistics, Digest of Education Statistics: 2012. Washington, DC: US Department of Education, 2012. nces.ed.gov.

in three rulings culminating with *Swann v. Charlotte-Mecklenburg Board of Education* in 1971, the High Court finally insisted that *Brown* required the elimination of racially-identifiable public schools. But just three years later, in *Milliken v. Bradley*, the Court refused to order interdistrict transportation of students in metropolitan Detroit in order to remedy stark inner-city racial isolation.

Milliken began a two-decade trend in Supreme Court jurisprudence that culminated in 1996 with *Missouri v. Jenkins*, a ruling that invalidated interdistrict

The realities of our failure to build a more thoroughly integrated society since the 1960s are vastly more complicated than an absence of appellate judicial will.

desegregation remedies in metropolitan Kansas City. Criticisms of the Supreme Court's post-*Swann* record are not as universally popular as are the complaints about its pre-1968 abdication. Yet liberals who blame the conservative majorities of the Burger and Rehnquist Courts for America's failure to pursue more extensive school integration over the past thirty years are simply choosing a politically convenient target.

Complex Reasons for Continuing Racial Isolation

The realities of our failure to build a more thoroughly integrated society since the 1960s are vastly more complicated than an absence of appellate judicial will. But a nuanced examination of that failure first requires consideration of the other primary contention of *Brown* critics, namely that African Americans should indeed be less supportive of integrationist ideals than they were during most of the 1960s. African American ambivalence about externally contrived integration efforts is not new, even if that disquiet is now more widely publicized. Indeed, such ambivalence is not limited to left-liberal African Americans such as Bell and Ogletree; one of the most powerful indictments of *Brown*'s integrationist zeal was penned by Justice Clarence Thomas in a concurring opinion in the 1996 *Missouri v. Jenkins* decision. In *Jenkins*, Justice Thomas complained that "it never ceases to amaze me that the courts are so willing to assume that anything that is predominantly black must be inferior."

Justice Thomas's criticism of *Brown* is memorable. "Mere de facto segregation (unaccompanied by discriminatory inequalities in educational resources) does not constitute a continuing harm after the end of de jure segregation," he wrote.

"Racial isolation" itself is not a harm; only state-enforced segregation is. After all, if separation itself is a harm, and if integration therefore is the only way that blacks can receive a proper education, then there must be something inferior about blacks. Under this theory, segregation injures blacks because blacks, when left on their own, cannot achieve. To my way of thinking, that conclusion is the result of a jurisprudence based on a theory of black inferiority.

Thomas took explicit aim at the widespread belief, one directly rooted in some of *Brown*'s own language, that "black students suffer an unspecified psychological harm from segregation that retards their mental and educational development." Instead, he asserted, "there is no reason to think that black students cannot learn as well when surrounded by members of their own race as when they are in an integrated environment."

Activists demonstrate in front of the US Supreme Court on the fiftieth anniversary of the *Brown v. Board of Education* decision. Many prominent voices of today have branded *Brown* a failure. **© Brendan Smialowski/Getty Images.**

Justice Thomas's argument may resonate far more positively among African Americans than his personal detractors would like to acknowledge. But Thomas's analytical goal with regard to *Brown* is one almost all constitutional conservatives now share: to embrace the famous ruling as a guidepost on the road to a "color blind" America, rather than wrestle with its integrationist assumptions. Judicial conservatives may still oppose most other constitutional innovations of the past fifty years, but ever since the civil rights revolution climaxed in 1964–1965, they have ardently insisted that *Brown*'s correct legacy entails eliminating all racial distinctions from government programs and policies.

Wanting to be on the "right side of history" may help explain judicial conservatives' change of tune on *Brown*. When combined with liberal disappointment and frustration, however, the result is a complete turnabout: conservatives now champion the quintessential "activist" decision, while liberals derogate and discount it.

Brown Inspired Great Societal Changes

Current academic dismissals of *Brown*'s historical importance are another odd and incongruous feature at fiftieth anniversary commemorations. Gerald Rosenberg's *The Hollow Hope* introduced that claim in the early 1990s. Michael Klarman's somewhat more muted argument asserts that *Brown* primarily aided the civil rights cause by generating a vitriolic and sometimes violent segregationist backlash that repulsed noncommittal whites and aided civil rights proponents.

But self-consciously revisionist contentions such as Klarman's attempt to demonstrate their novelty only at the price of significantly understating what a powerfully inspirational effect news of the *Brown* decision had on protest-minded African Americans. In the South, *Brown* stimulated increased grassroots protest in very short order. In Alabama, for example, JoAnn Gibson

> The paradoxical and erroneous claim that *Brown* somehow proves that landmark judicial rulings cannot fundamentally change a society by advancing human liberty [is] especially dubious.

Robinson, the Alabama State College professor who eighteen months later took the lead in calling for a boycott of Montgomery's municipal buses following the now-famous arrest of Rosa Parks, first threatened such a withdrawal of patronage in a letter to the city's mayor dated May 21, 1954, just four days after *Brown*. In July, another Montgomery activist, Reverend Solomon Seay, appeared before the state board of education to advocate the immediate integration of the University of Alabama. Two months after that, the Montgomery chapter of the NAACP petitioned for the desegregation of local schools and some two dozen African American children sought admission to an all-white elementary school.

One need not belabor the point by citing countless additional such examples, but the claim that *Brown* did not help spark greater black activism than otherwise would have occurred is not merely an abstruse historians' tussle. That argument helps advance a potentially potent political claim: that Supreme Court decisions "cannot fundamentally transform a nation," in Klarman's words, even in instances like *Brown* or *Baker v. Carr* (1962), the landmark reapportionment case.

Klarman and Rosenberg's minimizations of *Brown*, like similarly erroneous contentions that the abortion rights struggle in the United States would have fared better had the Supreme Court not handed down its far-reaching ruling in *Roe v. Wade* in 1973, argue against the political utility of constitutional reform litigation and judicial power. If *Brown*'s anniversary supplies an occasion for greater attention to such claims, then commemorations may have the deleterious effect of dissuading observers from enlisting in current or future constitutional reform crusades.

The paradoxical and erroneous claim that *Brown* somehow proves that landmark judicial rulings cannot fundamentally change a society by advancing human liberty looks especially dubious at a time when the Massachusetts Supreme Judicial Court's vindication of the right to marry in *Goodridge v. Department of Public Health* [2003] is offering full legal equality to gay and lesbian citizens for the first time in American history.

Diversity in Local Communities Remains a Challenge

But disproving wrong-headed academic fads about *Brown* is far easier than offering a full and nuanced answer for why racial separation and isolation remain so widespread in today's America. One new scholarly volume, Charles T. Clotfelter's *After Brown*, offers a rich statistical history of school desegregation ups and downs since 1954. Another recent title, Sheryll Cashin's *The Failures of Integration*, forcefully and persuasively identifies residential segregation as by far the largest, most influential reason for why American schools still exhibit such stark racial—and class—disparities.

Addressing the absence of racial and economic diversity in so many urban and suburban neighborhoods is a vastly greater challenge than critiquing conservative Supreme Court rulings of the past thirty years. Professor Cashin, who teaches at the Georgetown University Law Center and clerked for Justice Thurgood Marshall during his final year on the U.S. Supreme Court, expressly appreciates how dauntingly difficult a task her book outlines. But if public schools are to be more diverse and less segregated in twenty-five or fifty years than they are today, her analysis and prescription are highly cogent.

Only the private and public choices of tens of thousands of Americans, acting both individually and collectively, will be able to increase community diversity in this country's residential neighborhoods. Cashin's argument is one that some readers may dismiss as outlining a naively optimistic "mission impossible," but her call to action and civic engagement stands out sharply among the dyspeptic and pessimistic declarations that are too much in evidence at what should be an uplifting and reinvigorating time.

Brown v. Board of Education should rightfully be celebrated both as a landmark event on the continuing road to racial justice and as a judicial monument to how social reform can indeed be attained through constitutional litigation. That *Brown*'s vision of racial equality remains unfulfilled is no reason to either deny its huge contribution to the modern African American freedom struggle or its ongoing presence as a bright beacon for those who seek to use the law to advance human equality.

VIEWPOINT 3

School Segregation and the Achievement Gap Continue Almost Sixty Years After *Brown*

Lawrence D. Bobo

In the following viewpoint, a sociologist argues that the legacy of the 1954 *Brown v. Board of Education* decision remains unclear sixty years later. He admits that *Brown* altered the national culture and validated the political vision of African Americans. However, he writes, the continuing racial separation and gap in education achievement between black and white students shows that the promise of *Brown* is unfulfilled. He is troubled that equal educational opportunity still has not been reached. The complexities of law, politics, and racism must be addressed through a positive project of social change, he says. Lawrence D. Bobo is the W. E. B. Du Bois Professor of the Social Sciences at Harvard University, where he teaches sociology and African and African American studies. His research focuses on the intersection of social inequality, politics, and race.

SOURCE. Lawrence D. Bobo, "We Need a New Vision for the *Brown* Decision," TheRoot.com, May 16, 2013. Reproduced by permission.

Brown enshrines some transcendently important principles. But at the same time, with almost 60 years of hindsight, we can see plainly that it has a stunted legacy. That legacy is worthy of serious reflection and national soul-searching.

Sixty, of course, is one of the big ones. Even as life expectancy grows and our sense of what constitutes "middle age" expands, the big 6-0 signals a point for a special level of stock-taking and assessment. This is true for individuals and, I would suggest, for major cultural and legal landmarks like *Brown v. Board*.

There are those who think we should speak of *Brown* only in the most reverential and respectful tones. I understand why *Brown* occupies a deeply privileged and revered space in the African-American—indeed, American—cultural canon. The unanimous Earl Warren-led court declared that state-enforced racial segregation was unconstitutional. The practice was morally wrong and ran against the deepest American legal and political traditions of equality before the law and the fundamental dignity of the individual. As such, the decision repudiated a core feature of the Jim Crow system of racial oppression, still well-entrenched in 1954.

Brown's Positive Effects

Brown meant a good deal more than the dethroning of the "separate but equal" doctrine. With nearly 60 years of social evolution behind us, I think we can say that *Brown* played a key role in altering our national culture. It cast open bigotry and racism into profound disrepute. This is actually no small accomplishment. It means that for most Americans, including the great majority of white Americans, not being racist is a meaningful aspect of self-understanding and identity.

> The legacy of *Brown* is complex and murky when examined in full.

The *Brown* decision also validated the agency, the will and the political vision of black America, especially that of the black middle class. The work of the Legal Defense and Educational Fund of the NAACP, and leaders such as Charles Hamilton Houston, Thurgood Marshall, Constance Baker Motley and progressive white allies like Jack Greenberg, transformed not just the law but also the character of a nation and its culture. For all of these reasons, when the time comes, *Brown*'s jubilee should be celebratory.

Brown's Unfulfilled Promise

But the legacy of *Brown* is complex and murky when examined in full. On May 17, 1954, Marshall stood on the Supreme Court steps and confidently predicted that within five years there would be no more segregated schools in America. Yet we cannot today say that race has no bearing on which schools our children attend or on the quality of education that they are likely to receive. No. Some 59 years after the decision and following the distant waning of "massive resistance" and the rise and disappearance of the White Citizens' Council, America's public schools are about as segregated now as they were in 1980.

> "A large and worrisome gap in what black and white children get from schooling remains, particularly for those from low-income and poor communities."

A degree of ongoing segregation might be more tolerable if we could say that the black-white achievement gap had closed. To be sure, the disparity is not as great as it was at the time of the original ruling. However, a large and worrisome gap in what black and white children get from schooling remains, particularly for those from low-income and poor communities.

So, if one regarded the realization of genuinely equal educational opportunity as the promise of *Brown*, then

ACHIEVEMENT GAPS IN MATH AND READING BETWEEN WHITE AND BLACK PUBLIC SCHOOL STUDENTS AT GRADE 8

Amounts may not add up to 100 due to rounding.

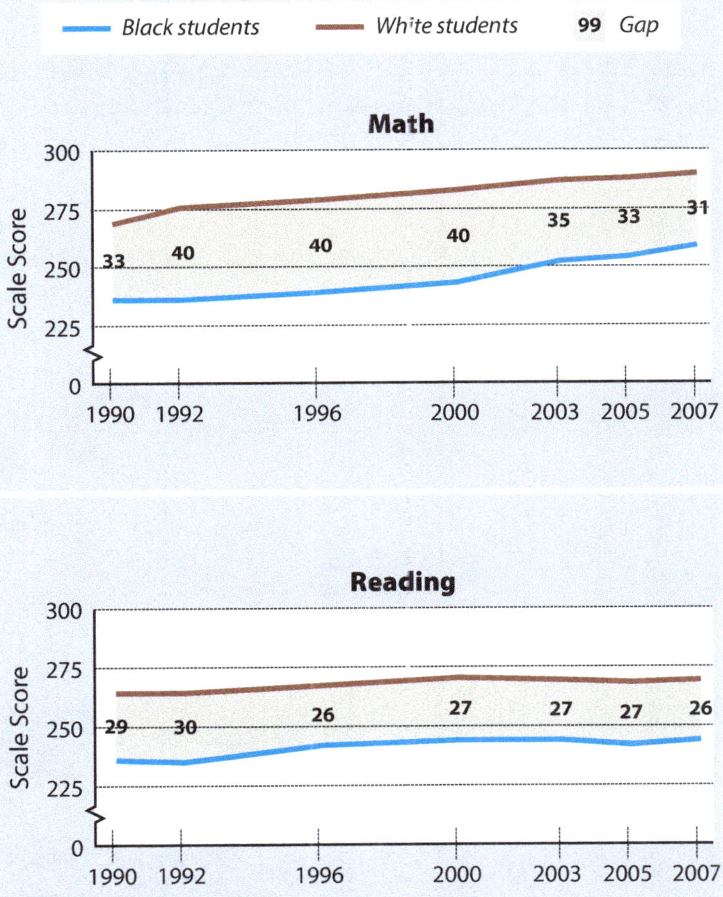

Data from: US Department of Education, Institute of Education Sciences, National Center for Education Statistics, National Assessment of Educational Progress (NAEP), various years, 1990–2007 Mathematics Assessments

Taken from: Alan Vanneman, et al. "Achievement Gaps: How Black and White Students in Public Schools Perform in Mathematics and Reading on the National Assessment of Educational Progress: Statistical Analysis," US Department of Education, National Center for Education Statistics, July 2009.

this part of its legacy remains unfulfilled. And, I would submit, troublingly so.

Brown Showed the Complexities of Racism

Let's cut one layer deeper: In many respects *Brown* was, at least initially, read as the death knell for racism in America. After all, it had taken away what many regarded as the central tenet of Jim Crow: legal, state-imposed segregation and discrimination. In so doing, the decision revealed the complexities of law, politics and, most of all, of racism.

With respect to the law, we learned that the language and logic of the ruling, especially as interpreted over the years, is increasingly taken to mean that the government cannot and should not pay any attention whatever to

At a demonstration in South Central Los Angeles marking the fiftieth anniversary of *Brown v. Board of Education*, signs on empty chairs signify the continuing segregation by race in educational and economic achievement. © **Hector Mata/AFP/Getty Images.**

race, even if its purpose is to achieve integration and greater equality. At least this is the tenor of interpretations flowing from Warren Burger to William Rehnquist and, now especially, to the John Roberts court.

> Rates of racial isolation in schools in too many places point in the wrong direction.

In politics, we learned that even authoritative Supreme Court rulings can neither ignore nor expect to be implemented in a straightforward fashion, given resistant white public opinion. We live in a time when desegregation orders are being lifted; when the Supreme Court, in the *Parents Involved* [*in Community Schools v. Seattle School District No. 1* (2007)] case, substantially invalidated voluntary plans to maintain integrated schools; and **rates of racial isolation in schools in too many places point in the wrong direction.**

Perhaps most all, we learned that racism was something far more complex, deeply rooted and malleable than was suggested by separate schools and "Whites Only" signs over drinking fountains and sections of restaurants. Racism involves a thickly interconnected set of economic and political arrangements, as well as cultural understandings and outlooks, that can only be transformed by a positive project of social change.

Vision Is Needed to Finally Defeat Inequality

It is that positive project that concerns me now as we begin to think about how to mark the coming 60th anniversary of *Brown*. The critical question for the black middle class and black leadership is: Are we content to continue watching the slow, ineluctable, steady dimming of the great spark of light the decision brought into the world? And I am not talking about a renewed push for school integration, though that is a very worthy project.

We should take this coming anniversary, and the year of planning that we have before us, as an occasion to talk, meet, think hard and organize on behalf of a renewed vision and renewed coalition building to deliver on the full promise of *Brown*. Our traditional civil rights organizations, as well as our churches, colleges and universities and progressive allies across the racial rainbow, need to focus on the unfilled legacy of *Brown*.

It was not wrong to have hoped, in 1954, that a thorough defeat of racial inequality and injustice was within our grasp. We know now that the reach of that legal victory was less than we had imagined and that our understanding of all that was needed to undo racial injustice was not nearly as robust as we thought. I don't know about you, but when that anniversary comes, I don't want symbolic gestures and hollow speeches. I want to celebrate *Brown* as part of an active plan to finish the work that Thurgood Marshall started.

VIEWPOINT 4

Black Schools Provided Better Educational Opportunities Before Desegregation

Jonathan Tilove

In the following viewpoint, a writer discusses a part of the legacy of the 1954 *Brown v. Board of Education* ruling that he believes has been absent from most narratives. The author reports on the important role of black schools before desegregation in African American achievement. The schools, he writes, had dedicated teachers, strong principals, order, discipline, and high expectations of their students. In fact, he writes, the limitations of segregation were turned into advantages by the teachers and the community. Many black schools were breeding grounds for high achieving African Americans of national renown, he states. Some African Americans lament that schools after *Brown* do not treat black children as being as capable as the white children, and the legacy of high achievement in black-only schools has

---

SOURCE. Jonathan Tilove, "In Black Schools Before *Brown*, Keys to Success," Newhouse News Services, April 28, 2004.

been lost. Jonathan Tilove, a journalist who has written extensively about race issues, is the author of *Along Martin Luther King: Travels on Black America's Main Street* and is the chief political writer of the *Austin American-Statesman*.

As America marks the 50th anniversary of the Supreme Court's *Brown v. Board of Education* decision, the ruling is celebrated as a freedom song, the death knell for legally segregated schools and, with them, an order of racial apartheid that dictated the rules of black-white relations in the American South and beyond.

But to many, *Brown*—handed down May 17, 1954—was also a dirge for something precious and irreplaceable: a network of black schools almost sacred to those they served and wholly devoted in their belief in black ability and pursuit of black advancement.

> Black communities, under the thumb and under the radar of oppression, created schools that imbued black children with a sense of confidence and possibility.

"*Brown* was turned against us. We lost our schools," says Elias Blake Jr., who graduated in 1947 from Risley High School in Brunswick, Ga., and credits it with transforming him from an indifferent student, sights set no higher than a job at the local hotel, into someone who became valedictorian of his college class and ultimately president of Clark College in Atlanta.

Absent from the standard telling of *Brown*: the superior education that many black schools provided is a source of fierce pride for alumni, and the subject of a growing body of scholarship.

A Mission to Tell the Stories of Black Schools

For those who knew or came to know these schools, recounting their story is a mission—to more truly and fully record history, to render thanks and give credit where due. It is a remarkable tale of how black communities, under the thumb and under the radar of oppression, created schools that imbued black children with a sense of confidence and possibility in the very midst of a system determined to limit them.

"They were not preparing their children for a segregated world. They were preparing their children for a world that did not exist, for an integrated world," says Vanessa Siddle Walker, an educational historian at Emory University.

Today, the schools' successes resonate with more than historical interest. In the decades since *Brown*, an American dilemma of legally sanctioned, separate and unequal education was replaced by a stubborn gap in black and white educational achievement, endlessly calibrated and worried over. *Brown*'s most profound irony may be that answers to closing the achievement gap lie buried in the history of the schools that *Brown*'s implementation destroyed.

Black Schools Engendered Excellence

Glittering amid the ruins, the answers are straightforward: Dedicated teachers. Strong principals. Order. Discipline. High expectations. Community and parental support. What is astonishing, Siddle Walker says, is how many black children attended schools during segregation that delivered on these objectives, and how few do so now.

As early as the 1970s, economist Thomas Sowell, now a senior fellow at the Hoover Institution at Stanford University, was writing about "patterns of black excellence" at segregated schools like Atlanta's Booker T. Washington, which produced Martin Luther King Jr.; Frederick Douglass in Baltimore, which produced Thurgood Marshall; McDonough 35 in New Orleans, which produced the first black state superintendent of schools

(California's Wilson Riles); and Paul Laurence Dunbar High School in Washington, D.C.

Dunbar, the first black high school in America, produced the first black Cabinet member (Robert C. Weaver); the first black general (Benjamin O. Davis); the discoverer of blood plasma (Charles R. Drew); the first black senator since Reconstruction (Edward W. Brooke, R-Mass.); Charles Hamilton Houston, the first special counsel to the NAACP and chief architect of the assault on Jim Crow that led to *Brown*; and Eleanor Holmes Norton, the District of Columbia delegate to Congress.

By 1899, students at Dunbar—then called the M Street School—scored higher on citywide tests than white students in Washington.

Lawrence Graves, class of 1940, recalls that his homeroom of 32 boys produced nine medical doctors, one dentist, three judges and four lawyers. "All the rest were educators," says Graves, a retired D.C. principal.

After *Brown*, Dunbar was not the same, and Graves, who at 82 still arranges alumni scholarships, says there is no way to recapture what was lost: "It was segregation. You had all these wonderful teachers who couldn't get jobs in other places. Circumstances have changed."

And yet, as Sowell wrote, the history of success needs to be remembered and understood at a time when public discussions of "quality education of black children proceed as if educational excellence were only a remote possibility, to be reached by futuristic experimental methods."

Segregation Was Key to the Experience

Most notable about the scholarship since Sowell is the rediscovery of exceptional black schools all across the landscape of segregated America. Hard data such as Sowell deployed in describing Dunbar are hard to come by. But descriptions are stunning in their sameness.

These were schools of unstinting discipline, order and respect. Of committed teachers and the most keen and caring mentorship. Of high and unyielding expectations. “People assumed you were first rate,” Graves says.

The schools were confident in the esteem in which they were held and the support they could expect at home. “There was no daylight between teachers and parents,” says Blake. “If you got punishment from a teacher, they sent a note home and you got a second punishment when you got there.”

Segregation imposed a unity of circumstance and purpose on black Americans.

“Today it’s a cliché, ‘it takes a village to raise a child.’ It’s just a slogan. But it was not a slogan in my day,” says Faustine Jones-Wilson, a former editor of the Journal of Negro Education, who in 1981 wrote about her alma mater in the book “A Traditional Model of Education Excellence: Dunbar High School of Little Rock, Arkansas.”

Segregation imposed a unity of circumstance and purpose on black Americans. “It was clear if you didn’t want to be a domestic servant or manual laborer, you had better learn something,” says Jones-Wilson, now retired outside Washington, D.C., where for a quarter-century she was a professor of education at Howard University.

Segregation was meant to limit black advancement, and the schools were supposed to do their part. But Siddle Walker says the black schools were tied together by a tight, if nearly invisible, national network of black educators, sharing ideas and strategies. The very neglect of the white powers allowed them unusual freedom. The genius of these schools, she says, was their ability to use that freedom to rewrite the debilitating script of segregation into one of uplift.

Blake recalls how Risley High School students built their own gymnasium. It was an act of self-help, he says, but also of cunning.

The students involved in the *Brown v. Board* case—from left, Vicki Henderson, Donald Henderson, Linda Brown (the 'Brown' of the case's name), James Emanuel, Nancy Todd, and Katherine Carper—pose for a portrait in 1953 in Topeka, Kansas. **© Carl Iwasaki/ Time Life Pictures/Getty Images.**

What the white superintendent and school board would see in that handmade gym were young blacks being trained for lives of manual labor. But, Blake says, "They were never brought into the main building where the laboratories were and where Mrs. Mollette was teaching Shakespeare, Thoreau, Emerson, Langston Hughes and Countee Cullen. They never saw any of that."

Risley High School, Blake says, was "doing college prep undercover."

A Wealth of Exceptional Teachers

And the stunting of black career opportunities lavished riches upon the ranks of black educators. Of the first nine principals of Dunbar, seven had degrees from Harvard, Oberlin, Dartmouth or Amherst, including the first black woman to receive a college degree (from Oberlin) and the first black man to graduate from Harvard. Carter Woodson, the renowned historian, taught at Dunbar.

> Black teachers in many Southern states were better educated than white teachers.

Even in little Beaufort, N.C., some 80 percent of the teachers at Queen Street High School held master's degrees, according to Lenwood Davis, a historian at Winston-Salem State University, who in 1996 wrote about the school, from which he graduated in 1957.

By 1950, Siddle Walker says, **black teachers in many Southern states were better educated than white teachers.** And because these Southern states paid for the graduate education of black students who went north to school, rather than admit them to their state universities, she found that many black educators returned home with Ivy League degrees.

Unfortunately, says Siddle Walker, that rich, coordinated network of able black educators no longer exists. "You can't go back," she says.

Separate Did Not Mean Inferior

In *Brown*, the Supreme Court unanimously held that "separate educational facilities are inherently unequal." In the public mind, black schools were judged inferior.

How, then, to explain the vibrant alumni groups formed by aging generations of graduates from Paul Laurence Dunbar, Booker T. Washington and Abraham Lincoln high schools in communities across the country, and their remarkably consistent memories of educational oases that each thought was a unique preserve?

For Siddle Walker, the unnerving contrast between the bright photos of engaged young people in yearbooks of the Caswell County Training School in her North Carolina hometown and the often listless black students she encountered in current-day schools led to her

> Typically desegregation resulted in closing black schools, dismissing black teachers, demoting black principals and dispersing black students.

prize-winning book, "Their Highest Potential: An African American School Community in the Segregated South."

Jones-Wilson's book was born in her curiosity about whether others shared her warm memories of Dunbar. They did.

Vivian Gunn Morris, a professor of education at the University of Memphis, and her husband, Curtis Morris, wrote two books about Trenholm High School in Tuscumbia, Ala., from which they graduated in 1959. It was torn down in 1969. When they talked to other alumni, "we were floored" by the depth of feeling, she says. "People were tearing and crying."

Typically desegregation resulted in closing black schools, dismissing black teachers, demoting black principals and dispersing black students from places where they had ruled the roost to white schools where they arrived as unwelcome strangers.

Black life in Tampa, Fla., revolved around two high schools—Middleton and Blake—both closed in the 1971 desegregation of Hillsborough County schools. "It was bad. It was terrible. More than anything, it was unbelievable," says Fred Hearns, a 1966 Middleton graduate, founder of its alumni association, and now Tampa's acting director of community affairs. "What we thought is that they would improve our school and bus in some white kids."

Instead, black children were scattered across 11 different high schools. (In recent years, new Middleton and Blake high schools were opened in response to demand from Tampa's black community.)

Bitterness About What Was Lost with Integration

In his 1994 book, "Along Freedom Road," historian David Cecelski told the story of how blacks in coastal

Hyde County, N.C., boycotted schools for a year in the late 1960s to protest a desegregation plan that would have closed their community's two historically black schools.

Cecelski says that when he talks to black audiences of a certain age, "I'm still always taken off guard by the depth of bitterness" about the loss of their schools. "I'm always asking myself how much is grounded in the strengths of those schools—and there is no question about it, that is real—and how much is grounded in what they see as the mistreatment and the damage done to African-American children in the schools today."

Blake today lives in Washington, D.C., where he remains active on issues of educational equity. "You look at any high school in this country," he says. "You will see that the faculties in those high schools do not believe that black children are as capable as white children."

He continues, "If we had kept control of all those high schools in the South there would have been no way that 20, 30, 40 percent of the students would have been classified in the lowest tracks, in special education and as mentally retarded.

"I mean, there is no way you can put an educator of my generation and those who educated me and those who we educated in a classroom and classify that many students as unable to meet the standards."

VIEWPOINT 5

Forced School Busing Caused Racial Turmoil in Boston

Bridget Murphy

The following viewpoint reports on the lasting effects of busing in Boston. In many areas, school integration was achieved by assigning students to schools based on demographic formulas. When schools were not in their neighborhoods, students would need to be transported there on buses, sometimes long distances and sometimes into neighborhoods or schools that did not welcome them. The author maintains that the experience of forced busing in Boston was a painful one for the students, and there are ongoing efforts to learn from their experiences. Although not all bused students experienced bias, for others the effect of the trauma has lingered, she writes. Bridget Murphy is a writer for the *Huffington Post*.

SOURCE. Bridget Murphy, "Effects of Desegregation Busing Linger in Boston," *Huffington Post*, April 7, 2013.

Last fall [2012], Ginnette Powell traveled from her home in Boston's Dorchester section to her old middle school in South Boston—a journey of just two miles, but one that covered a huge emotional distance. Finally, she was able to leave the painful past behind.

Powell endured the explosive battle over desegregation in Boston in the 1970s. Tears come to her eyes when she talks about how it took her decades to return to the place where she never felt safe as an African-American seventh-grader.

"It was scary because of what you were going into, getting bricks thrown at your bus. I remember the bus windows being broken," said Powell, now 48.

"People of different races and economic classes [should] learn from the city's busing past so they can fight together for access to quality schools."

Nearly four decades later, Powell's native city also is still working to move forward from the legacy of the school busing crisis. Last year, Mayor Thomas Menino created an advisory group whose aim was to work toward putting students back in neighborhood schools. And last month, school officials agreed to do away with the last vestiges of the desegregation-based school assignment system, beginning in 2014.

But raw feelings remain from that divisive time. And to explore and mend the divisions, the nonprofit Union of Minority Neighborhoods has been holding public story circles across Boston where participants like Powell can open up about their own experiences.

Learning from Bused Students' Experiences

Organizers hope the airing of voices will help people of different races and economic classes learn from the city's busing past so they can fight together for access to

quality schools for all students. Project director Donna Bivens said the exercises are designed to be about listening and discussing, but not judging each other's stories.

"I think that we can't move forward, looking at how to improve our schools and access to our schools without looking at how the past impacted the present," said Elaine Ng, executive director of the Boston Chinatown Neighborhood Center, which hosted the story circle where Powell described her visit back to her old school.

As the daughter of Chinese immigrants, Ng learned to speak English as a kindergarten student in a Boston public school. But after her family moved from Chinatown to a white neighborhood in 1976, students threw stones at her when she walked to school. Ng said one of her frustrations is that people don't recognize all the ripple effects busing had.

"It didn't matter whether or not you were on a bus," she said. "Racial tensions in the city were just really high."

The Painful Experience of Busing

The uproar started in 1974, when a federal judge imposed busing after a lawsuit claimed black students were getting lower-quality education than children who attended mostly white schools. Black students were bused to schools in white areas, and white students went to black neighborhoods. The National Guard was called in amid demonstrations and riots; school buses got police escorts.

> The busing conflict [is viewed] as a struggle between people of different classes, not just races.

The unrest continued for years. In 1976, a news photographer caught a white teenager attempting to spear a black man with an American flag during a busing protest outside City Hall. In 1979, 15-year-old black football player Darryl Williams was left paralyzed by a white sniper's bullet during a high school game.

Police escort school buses in Boston, Massachusetts, in 1974. Forced school busing was a traumatic experience for the city. **© AP Photo/Frank Curtin.**

Alexander Lynn, a 60-year-old African-American, was a young teacher at the beginning of the busing crisis. Later, he worked as a union organizer.

He was among several others, including Cassie Quinlan and Kevin Davis, who participated in the story circle with Powell.

Lynn said a white police officer once put a gun to his head and accused him of stealing a white child's bicycle after officers stopped him in a mostly white neighborhood. But when police found out he was a teacher, he said, they apologized and returned his bicycle.

He views the busing conflict as a struggle between people of different classes, not just races, and said he had the protection of whites as he lobbied for unions in South Boston in the same era.

A Bus Driver's Experience

Quinlan, who is white, drove one of the buses that took black students from the city's Roxbury section to high school in Charlestown. When she pulled up to the curb with a police escort, at least 100 white protesters would be lined up. Police would have to make a wall at the bus door so students could get into school.

"The black kids, they were nervous . . . ," said Quinlan, now 69. "I used to wish that somebody would smile and wave good morning. No, there was none of that."

Quinlan recalled returning to Charlestown in the early 1980s for a field trip. Then, she saw students of all races mixing together.

"I cried when I drove away, when I saw this, how much change had happened," she said.

> 'I had no control as a child being bused.'

Quinlan said her experiences opened her own eyes to black culture, and she became the first white member of a black gospel choir at a local university.

Davis, a 50-year-old African-American, said he was bused to Boston's Brighton section in 1976. Davis said neighborhood kids had paved the way at the mostly white school by then, and he didn't experience bias.

Trauma Lingers Years Later

But as a substance abuse counselor in Roxbury near where he grew up, Davis said many clients have said busing-related trauma put them on a path to addiction. He's heard stories from black clients about how white police officers who were in schools called them names; others have confessed that they threw rocks at white students.

Some dropped out of school to avoid conflicts that came with busing.

"For a lot of people this has never been closed. This is still open. The pain that they feel has never been addressed," Davis said.

But for story circle participants like Powell, talking about busing has been healing, as was her trip to South Boston.

"It's sort of making myself whole . . . ," she said. "I had no control as a child being bused, but as an adult I can go into these spaces."

VIEWPOINT 6

The Fight for Racial Balance in Schools Is Still Relevant

David L. Kirp

In the following viewpoint, a public policy and education expert writes that recent efforts to improve education outcomes have ignored, and sometimes undermined, the benefits of racial integration. In his view, a 2007 US Supreme Court decision may undo the progress caused by the 1954 *Brown v. Board of Education* decision. He cites research that indicates integrated schools benefit students of all races and encourages renewed policies for school integration as a way to improve schools. David L. Kirp is a professor of public policy at the University of California, Berkeley and the author of *Kids First: Five Big Ideas for Transforming Children's Lives and America's Future* and *Improbable Scholars: The Rebirth of a Great American School System and a Strategy for American Education*.

SOURCE. David Kirp, "Making Schools Work," *New York Times*, May 19, 2012. Reproduced by permission.

Amid the ceaseless and cacophonous debates about how to close the achievement gap, we've turned away from one tool that has been shown to work: school desegregation. That strategy, ushered in by the landmark 1954 Supreme Court decision in *Brown v. Board of Education*, has been unceremoniously ushered out, an artifact in the museum of failed social experiments. The Supreme Court's ruling that racially segregated schools were "inherently unequal" shook up the nation like no other decision of the 20th century. Civil rights advocates, who for years had been patiently laying the constitutional groundwork, cheered to the rafters, while segregationists mourned "Black Monday" and vowed "massive resistance." But as the anniversary was observed this past week on May 17 [2012], it was hard not to notice that desegregation is effectively dead. In fact, we have been giving up on desegregation for a long time. In 1974, the Supreme Court rejected [in *Milliken v. Bradley*] a metropolitan integration plan, leaving the increasingly black cities to fend for themselves.

> To the current reformers, integration is at best an irrelevance and at worst an excuse to shift attention away from shoddy teaching. But a spate of research says otherwise.

A generation later, public schools that had been ordered to integrate in the 1960s and 1970s became segregated once again, this time with the blessing of a new generation of justices. And five years ago, a splintered court delivered the coup de grâce when it decreed [in *Parents Involved in Community Schools v. Seattle School District No. 1* (2007)] that a school district couldn't voluntarily opt for the most modest kind of integration—giving parents a choice of which school their children would attend and treating race as a tiebreaker in deciding which children would go to the most popular schools. In the perverse logic of Chief Justice John G. Roberts Jr., this amounted to "discriminating among

At a newly-integrated school in Tennessee in 1955, students chat before the start of class. Many argue that the racial integration in schools has provided many benefits to people of all races. © **Underwood Archives/Getty Images.**

individual students based on race." That's bad history, which, as Justice Stephen G. Breyer wrote in an impassioned dissent, "threaten[s] the promise of *Brown*."

Racial Integration Has Many Positive Effects

To the current reformers, integration is at best an irrelevance and at worst an excuse to shift attention away from shoddy teaching. But a spate of research says otherwise. The experience of an integrated education made all the difference in the lives of black children—and in the lives of their children as well. These economists' studies consistently conclude that African-American students who attended integrated schools fared better academically than those left behind in segregated schools. They were more likely to graduate from high school and attend and graduate from college; and, the longer they spent attending integrated schools, the better they did. What's more, the fear that white children would suffer, voiced by opponents of integration, proved groundless. Between 1970 and 1990, the black-white gap in educational attainment shrank—not because white youngsters did worse but because black youngsters did better.

Not only were they more successful in school, they were more successful in life as well. A 2011 study by the Berkeley public policy professor Rucker C. Johnson concludes that black youths who spent five years in desegregated schools have earned 25 percent more than those who never had that opportunity. Now in their 30s and 40s, they're also healthier—the equivalent of being seven years younger.

A Transformative Experience

Why? For these youngsters, the advent of integration transformed the experience of going to school. By itself, racial mixing didn't do the trick, but it did mean that the fate of black and white students became intertwined. School systems that had spent a pittance on all-black schools were now obliged to invest considerably more on African-American students' education after the schools became integrated. Their classes were smaller and better equipped. They included children from better-off families, a factor that the landmark 1966 [National Center for Educational Statistics] Equality of Educational Opportunity study had shown to make a significant difference in academic success. What's more, their teachers and parents held them to higher expectations. That's what shifted the arc of their lives.

Professor Johnson takes this story one big step further by showing that the impact of integration reaches to the next generation. These youngsters—the grandchildren of *Brown*—are faring better in school than those whose parents attended racially isolated schools.

Parents Involved in Community Schools v. Seattle School District No. 1

The Seattle School District allowed students to apply to any high school in the district. Since certain schools often became oversubscribed when too many students chose them as their first choice, the district used a system of tiebreakers to decide which students would be admitted to the popular schools. The second most important tiebreaker was a racial factor intended to maintain racial diversity. If the racial demographics of any school's student body deviated by more than a predetermined number of percentage points from those of Seattle's total student population (approximately 40 percent white and 60 percent non-white), the racial tiebreaker went into effect. At a particular school either whites or non-whites could be favored for admission depending on which race would bring the racial balance closer to the goal.

A non-profit group, Parents Involved in Community Schools, sued the district, arguing that the racial tiebreaker violated the Equal Protection Clause of the Fourteenth Amendment as well as the Civil Rights Act of 1964 and Washington state law. . . .

By a 5-4 vote, the Court applied a "strict scrutiny" framework [meaning that the law must be justified by a compelling governmental interest, be narrowly tailored to achieve that interest, and be the least restrictive way to achieve the interest] and found the district's racial tiebreaker plan uncon-

Despite the Horatio Alger myth that anyone can make it in America, moving up the socioeconomic ladder is hard going: children from low-income families have only a 1 percent chance of reaching the top 5 percent of the income distribution, versus children of the rich, who have about a 22 percent chance.

Overcoming the Burdens of Poverty

But many of the poor black children who attended desegregated schools in the 1970s escaped from poverty, and their offspring have maintained that advantage.

stitutional under the Equal Protection Clause of the Fourteenth Amendment. Chief Justice John Roberts wrote in the plurality opinion that "The way to stop discrimination on the basis of race is to stop discriminating on the basis of race." . . . [The Court also found that] the District's plan involved no individualized consideration of students, and it employed a very limited notion of diversity ("white" and "non-white"). The District's goal of preventing racial imbalance did not meet the Court's standards for a constitutionally legitimate use of race: "Racial balancing is not transformed from 'patently unconstitutional' to a compelling state interest simply by relabeling it 'racial diversity.'" The plans also lacked the narrow tailoring that is necessary for race-conscious programs. The Court held that the District's tiebreaker plan was actually targeted toward demographic goals and not toward any demonstrable educational benefit from racial diversity. The District also failed to show that its objectives could not have been met with non–race-conscious means. In a separate opinion concurring in the judgment, Justice Kennedy agreed that the District's use of race was unconstitutional but stressed that public schools may sometimes consider race to ensure equal educational opportunity.

SOURCE: "Parents Involved in Community Schools v. Seattle School District No. 1," *The Oyez Project at IIT Chicago-Kent College of Law, March 29, 2014. www.oyez.org.*

Of course desegregation was not a cure-all. While the achievement gap and the income gap narrowed during the peak era of desegregation, white children continued to do noticeably better. That's to be expected, for schools can't hope to overcome the burdens of poverty or the lack of early education, which puts poor children far behind their middle-class peers before they enter kindergarten. And desegregation was too often implemented in ham-handed fashion, undermining its effectiveness. Adherence to principle trumped good education, as students were sent on school buses simply to achieve the numerical goal of racial balance. Understandably, that aroused opposition, and not only among those who thought desegregation was a bad idea. Despite its flaws, integration is as successful an educational strategy as we've hit upon. As the U.C.L.A. political scientist Gary Orfield points out, "On some measures the racial achievement gaps reached their low point around the same time as the peak of black-white desegregation in the late 1980s."

If we're serious about improving educational opportunities, we need to revisit the abandoned policy of school integration.

And in the 1990s, when the courts stopped overseeing desegregation plans, black students in those communities seem to have done worse. The failure of the No Child Left Behind [Act of 2001] regimen to narrow the achievement gap offers the sobering lesson that closing underperforming public schools, setting high expectations for students, getting tough with teachers and opening a raft of charter schools isn't the answer. If we're serious about improving educational opportunities, we need to revisit the abandoned policy of school integration.

In theory it's possible to achieve a fair amount of integration by crossing city and suburban boundaries or opening magnet schools attractive to both minority and white students. But the hostile majority on the Supreme Court and the absence of a vocal pro-integration constituency make integration's revival a near impossibility.

VIEWPOINT 7

Continuing Racial Imbalance in Schools Is Not a Problem

Abigail Thernstrom and Stephan Thernstrom

In the following viewpoint, two conservative academics counter the argument that rectifying racial imbalance in schools is a worthy goal. They write that racial balance in schools is not a reasonable measurement of educational progress for a number of reasons. They explain that balance, regardless of how it's defined, is not achievable in every school because each community is different. Furthermore, they argue, racially uniform neighborhoods are normal and even desirable for minorities. They acknowledge that the racial gap in academic achievement is the most important source of racial inequality. However, they contend, low educational achievement isn't rooted in the racial make-up of the student body in poorly performing schools. Abigail Thernstrom is the vice-chair of the US Commission on Civil Rights and an adjunct scholar at the American Enterprise Institute, a conservative think tank. Stephan Thernstrom is the

---

SOURCE. Abigail Thernstrom and Stephan Thernstrom, "Have We Overcome?," *Commentary*, vol. 118, no. 4, November 2011, p. 49. Reprinted from Commentary, November 2011, by permission.

Winthrop Research Professor of History at Harvard University. They are coauthors of *No Excuses: Closing the Racial Gap in Learning* and *America in Black and White: One Nation, Indivisible*.

Is America still "segregated"? In our deeply divided national conversation on race, the question endures, and it was raised again last spring [2004] by the 50th-anniversary celebrations of *Brown v. Board of Education*. Did that landmark decision by the Supreme Court promise much and deliver little? . . .

It is easy to forget how far we have come over the past 50 years. When *Brown* was decided, there was no interracial contact at all in the schools of the South, the region where most African-American children lived. Even ten years later, only a little more than 1 percent of black public-school students in the eleven ex-Confederate states had any white classmates. But state-sanctioned segregation did come to an end. No American child still attends a school that is legally restricted to other pupils of the same race. No state laws send the message (as Justice John Marshall Harlan witheringly put it, dissenting in *Plessy v. Ferguson*, the 1896 precedent overturned by *Brown*) that African-Americans "are so inferior and degraded that they cannot be allowed to sit" with whites. Today, the typical black youngster attends a school that is only about half-black—an extraordinary change in a half-century.

Or is it? The most curious aspect of the anniversary of *Brown* last spring was the hand-wringing that accompanied so much of the celebration. Paul Vallas, Philadelphia's education chief, lamented that "we're still wrestling with the same issues" today as in 1954. Newsweek opined that "*Brown*, for all its glow, is something of a bust." For the Harvard law professor Charles Ogletree, "the evil that *Brown* sought to eliminate—segregation—is still with us." His verdict was shared by the *Washington Post* columnist Colbert King. "Segregation has found its way back—if, indeed, it ever left some schools," he wrote. "To be sure, today's racial separation is not sanctioned by law. But in terms of racial isolation, the effect is much the same."

Flaws in the Calculation of "Racial Balance"

The charge that our schools, in particular, remain segregated—or have been "resegregated"—rests heavily on the work of the social scientist Gary Orfield and his

TRENDS IN EDUCATIONAL ATTAINMENT

Percentage of Americans aged 25 to 29 with a Bachelor's degree or higher

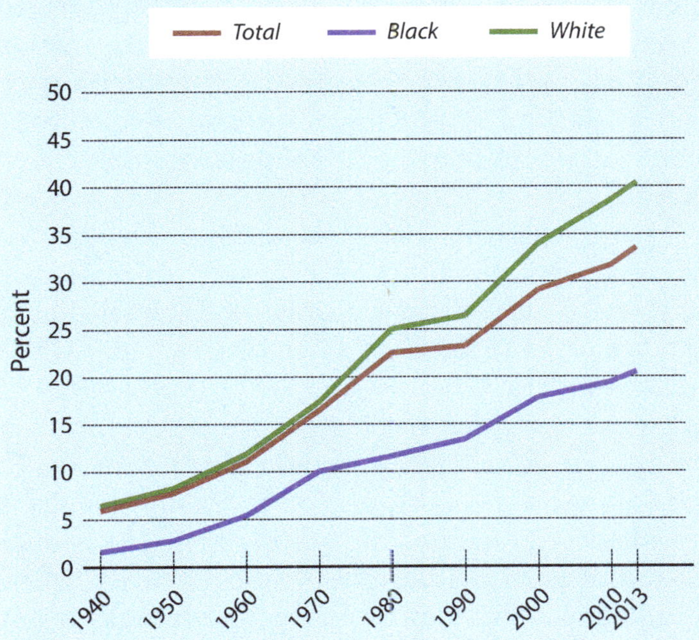

Taken from: National Center for Education Statistics, Table 104.20, Digest of Education Statistics 2013. Washington, DC: US Department of Education, October 2013. http://nces.ed.gov.

colleagues at Harvard's Civil Rights Project, whose findings are regularly and uncritically reported in the media. In his most recent report, *Brown at 50: King's Dream or Plessy's Nightmare?*, Orfield concedes that legally enforced, de-jure segregation has disappeared, but, he argues, the effect of the constitutional victory has turned out to be small.

Using data from the National Center for Education Statistics, Orfield has created an "index of exposure" to measure the extent to which minority students now attend school with white classmates. The findings alarm him. In 2001–02, the typical black youngster attended a school that was 54-percent black and just 31-percent white, with other minorities making up the remainder. The results for Hispanic students are much the same: Hispanics typically form a majority and whites constitute just 28 percent of their classmates. By Orfield's reckoning, the level of "segregation" in the nation's schools has returned to that of 1968. For America's minorities, Martin Luther King, Jr.'s dream of equality has become, it would seem, a "nightmare" from our racist past. . . .

Photo on following page: African American students in Marion, Alabama—a majority African American community—attend an event celebrating the election of the first black US president in 2009. Some Americans argue that it is normal for communities and local schools to self-segregate by race. © **AP Photo/Dave Martin.**

What then is the "right" proportion of whites? According to Orfield's index of exposure, a "segregated" school is a so-called "majority-minority" school—that is, one in which more than half the students are non-whites. Orfield's measure is not the one used by most social scientists who study the distribution of different racial and ethnic groups in schools, occupations, and housing. The standard measure is known as an index of dissimilarity or imbalance. It does not ask whether there are "enough" whites in a particular school—"enough" being defined by Orfield as more than 50 percent—but looks instead at the school's racial composition in relation to the wider community. Thus, if the school population in Boston is 15-percent white and 48-percent black, and that is also the rough proportion in every school, there is no

> A deeper question is whether even the conventional measure of racial 'balance' is an appropriate way to gauge racial progress in education.

cause for concern, even though the white percentage in each school is small. . . .

But a deeper question is whether even the conventional measure of racial "balance" is an appropriate way to gauge racial progress in education. Should we really expect every school in a city to reflect that city's overall racial composition? In a footnote to *Brown*, concerning implementation, the Justices told the contending parties to devise plans that, while eliminating segregation, still respected "the limits set by normal geographic school districting." But unless every neighborhood has the same racial composition—a pattern that no American city even approximates—drawing "normal geographic" districts will inevitably produce schools in which one group or another is disproportionately represented. . . .

There is no denying that American blacks often live in their own residential enclaves, especially in our big cities. But the same is true of whites and of every other racial and ethnic group—Jews, Chinese, Cambodians, Cubans, Arabs. Such racial and ethnic clustering means that a third of non-Asian minorities attend schools that are less than 10-percent white. And even though whites constitute just over 60 percent of the nation's schoolchildren, the average white student goes to a school that is 80-percent white.

But why should we expect identical proportions of blacks and whites to live in each and every, neighborhood? People like to live near others with whom they identify, and the schools mirror their choices. When asked about their residential preferences, only about 5 percent of blacks said they wished to live on an entirely or almost entirely white block. The vast majority preferred neighborhoods that were half or more than half African-American—in other words, neighborhoods in which the black concentration was "disproportionately" high. According to the 2000 census, this happens to correspond closely to the actual distribution of black city-dwellers.

> It is only natural that people should sort themselves out in urban space along lines of race as well as of religion and social class.

Community Segregation Is Natural

In a complex, heterogeneous society, **it is only natural that people should sort themselves out in urban space along lines of race as well as of religion and social class.** This pattern was firmly established in the U.S. by the European immigrants who landed in the cities of the North in the 19th and early 20th centuries. The sociologists who studied these settlements recognized the important social functions served by "Little Italies" and "Poletowns."

The history of America's black "ghettos" is, of course, another matter—at least in part. If residential clusters of immigrants long reflected the preferences of the immigrant groups themselves, concentrations of blacks were largely the result of the determination of whites to exclude them. Among the tools used to achieve this end were covenants that restricted the rental and sale of property, "gentlemen's agreements" among real-estate agents, and harassment of blacks who moved into white neighborhoods.

Even so, however, brute exclusion was never the entire story. In some measure, black migrants from the South (like Europeans from abroad) were choosing to live in sections of cities like Chicago where other blacks, who had arrived before them, were residing. They found apartments where their kin or friends lived and where they felt culturally at home. Nevertheless, most social scientists at the time resolutely dismissed the possibility that American blacks made residential choices based on cultural comfort.

This was part and parcel of a larger syndrome: many scholars rejected the very idea that American blacks possessed a distinctive, positive identity of their own. . . .

Blacks are no longer a uniquely stigmatized racial minority. They are becoming, in important respects, just another American ethnic group (as the widespread embrace of the hyphenated term "African-American" suggests). To be sure, average black family income is lower than that of whites and Asians. Nevertheless, the persistence of predominantly black neighborhoods is no more surprising—or troubling—than the clustering of Jews in, say, Brooklyn, or of Chinese in Chinatown.

Racial Make-Up Does Not Reflect Quality

When reporters, activists, and social scientists describe today's urban landscape as "segregated," they imply that a high concentration of blacks or Latinos—unlike high concentrations of other groups—diminishes the quality of life in these communities. Douglas S. Massey and Nancy A. Denton, the authors of American Apartheid, argue that the current level of racial clustering in urban neighborhoods "systematically undermines the social and economic well-being of blacks in the United States."

> The racial mix in a school does not determine the quality of the children's education.

Can this be true? Is race itself the deciding factor in the problems of these communities? Does the same analysis extend to heavily black suburbs like Prince George's County, Maryland—settings to which high-income blacks, with plenty of choices, have eagerly gravitated? Many well-meaning liberals still find it impossible to see anything but discrimination when black families are not randomly distributed across the residential landscape. But there is nothing wrong with racial and ethnic enclaves—indeed, there is much that is right with them—so long as blacks are no longer barred from neighborhoods in which they would prefer to live.

Similarly, labeling schools with few whites as "segregated" implies that learning there is likely to be compromised. Although total racial isolation as a way of life is highly undesirable, **the racial mix in a school does not determine the quality of the children's education.** Those who repeat the charge of segregation like a mantra seem to believe that the central problem with urban schools is that they are not white enough—a conviction that itself should cause some discomfort within the civil-rights community. As Justice Clarence Thomas wrote in a 1995 desegregation decision, "It never ceases to amaze me that the courts are so willing to assume that anything that is predominantly black must be inferior." . . .

Segregation Does Not Cause Education Problems

It hardly needs saying that all is not well in the schools that black and Hispanic children attend, whether in inner cities or in affluent suburbs. The racial gap in academic achievement has become the most important source of ongoing racial inequality. Equal skills and knowledge mean equal earnings, and the typical black or Hispanic youngster is leaving high school with junior-high-school skills. But to invoke "segregation" as the cause of this gap, when it plainly is not, is to provide just one more excuse for the cultural and educational failures at the root of this problem—and for the schools that fail to confront them.

Those who recall what life was like for blacks in the Deep South before *Brown v. Board of Education* and the 1964 Civil Rights Act should be outraged by the equation of racial imbalance with segregation. The black children who broke the color-line in Jim Crow schools—the children who faced white mobs spewing insults and brandishing sticks—showed extraordinary courage in the face of state-sanctioned racism. Advocates of racially balanced schools are not engaged in a remotely similar fight. In claiming otherwise, they not only rob the civil-rights movement of its achievement, but turn our eyes toward the wrong prize—schools that look right rather than schools in which children, whatever their color, are truly learning.

VIEWPOINT 8

African Americans Are Not to Blame for the Failures of *Brown*

Michael Eric Dyson

On the fiftieth anniversary of the 1954 *Brown v. Board of Education* decision, African American comedian, educator, and author Bill Cosby gave a controversial and widely disseminated speech. In the speech, Cosby said that African Americans could no longer blame segregation or government institutions for the continuing cycle of black poverty and the racial achievement gap. The following viewpoint is part of a response to the Cosby speech by an academic, author, and radio host. The author counters Cosby's arguments that lack of personal responsibility and amoral behavior are to blame to the failures of the *Brown* decision. He cites the economic, social, and structural barriers that continue to hold back African American achievement. He writes that any failures of *Brown* to instigate sufficient change are due to a lack of adequate investment in the educational infrastructure in areas where poor African American students

---

SOURCE. Michael Eric Dyson, *Is Bill Cosby Right?* New York: Basic Civitas, 2005. Reproduced by permission.

live. In fact, he says, the issues that Cosby and others point out are really a rift related to class and social status. Michael Eric Dyson is a professor of sociology at Georgetown University and the author of *Is Bill Cosby Right? Or Has the Black Middle Class Lost Its Mind?* and *Come Hell or High Water: Hurricane Katrina and the Color of Disaster*.

"Do you view Bill Cosby as a race traitor?" journalist Paula Zahn bluntly asked me on her nighttime television show [*Paula Zahn Now* on CNN].

Zahn was referring to the broadside the entertainer had launched against irresponsible black parents who are poor and their delinquent children. Cosby's rebuke came in a May 2004 speech on the fiftieth anniversary of the landmark Supreme Court decision *Brown v. Board of Education*. Not content with a one-off tirade, Cosby since then has bitterly and visibly crusaded against the declining morality and bad behavior of poor blacks. Six months into his battle, Zahn snagged the comic legend turned cultural warrior for his first in-depth interview. Cosby clarified his comments and reinforced his position. No, he wasn't wrong to air the black community's dirty laundry. Yes, he would ratchet up the noise and pace of his racial offensive. And he surely didn't give a damn about what white folk thought about his campaign or what nefarious uses they might make of his public diatribe. One could see it on Cosby's face: This is war, the stakes are high and being polite or politically correct simply won't do. . . .

Cosby's remarks betray seething class warfare in black America that has finally boiled over to the general public. It is that general public, especially white social critics and other prophets of black ethical erosion, that has been eager for Cosby's dispatches from the tortured front of black class war. Cosby's comments let many of these whites off the hook. If what Cosby says is true, then critics who have said the same, but who courted charges of racism, are vindicated. There's nothing like a formerly poor black multimillionaire bashing poor blacks to lend credence to the ancient assaults they've endured from the dominant culture. . . .

Structural Racism Is at the Root of Ongoing Problems

Cosby's overemphasis on personal responsibility, not structural features, wrongly locates the source of poor black suffering—and by implication its remedy—in the lives of the poor. When you think the problems are personal, you think the solutions are the same. If only the poor were willing to work harder, act better, get educated, stay out of jail and parent more effectively, their problems would go away. It's hard to argue against any of these things in the abstract; in principle such suggestions sound just fine. But one could do all of these things and still be in bad shape at home, work or school. For instance, Cosby completely ignores shifts in the economy that give value to some work while other work, in the words of William Julius Wilson, "disappears." In our high-tech, high-skilled economy where low-skilled work is being scaled back, phased out, exported, or severely undercompensated, all the right behavior in the world won't create better jobs with more pay. And without such support, all the goals that Cosby expresses for the black poor are not likely to become reality. If the rigidly segregated educational system continues to miserably fail poor blacks by failing to prepare their children for the world of work, then admonitions to "stay in school" may ring hollow.

"If the rigidly segregated educational system continues to miserably fail poor blacks . . . admonitions to 'stay in school' may ring hollow."

Bill Cosby's "Pound Cake Speech"

Following are excerpts from a transcription of a speech given by Bill Cosby at Constitution Hall in Washington, DC, on May 17, 2004.

Fifty percent drop-out rate, I'm telling you, and people in jail, and women having children by five, six different men. Under what excuse? "I want somebody to love me." And as soon as you have it, you forget to parent. Grandmother, mother, and great grandmother in the same room, raising children, and the child knows nothing about love or respect of any one of the three of them. All this child knows is "gimme, gimme, gimme." These people want to buy the friendship of a child, and the child couldn't care less. Those of us sitting out here who have gone on to some college or whatever we've done, we still fear our parents. And these people are not parenting. They're buying things for the kid—$500 sneakers—for what? They won't buy or spend $250 on *Hooked on Phonics* [reading education materials]. . . .

Looking at the incarcerated, these are not political criminals. These are people going around stealing Coca Cola. People getting shot in the back of the head over a piece of pound cake! Then we all run out and are outraged: "The cops shouldn't have shot him." What the hell was he doing with the pound cake in his hand? I wanted a piece of pound cake just as bad as anybody else. And I looked at it and I had no money. And something called parenting said if you get caught with it you're going to embarrass your mother." Not, "You're going to get your butt kicked." No. "You're going to embarrass your mother." "You're going

In this light, the imprisonment of black people takes on political consequence. Cosby may be right that most black folk in jail are not "political prisoners," but it doesn't mean that their imprisonment has not been politicized. Given the vicious way blacks have been targeted for incarceration, Cosby's comments about poor blacks who end up in jail are dangerously naïve and empirically wrong. . . .

Cosby also slights the economic, social, political and other structural barriers that poor black parents are up to embarrass your family." If you knock that girl up, you're going to have to run away because it's going to be too embarrassing for your family. . . . We are not parenting.

Ladies and gentlemen, listen to these people. They are showing you what's wrong. People putting their clothes on backwards. Isn't that a sign of something going on wrong? Are you not paying attention? People with their hat on backwards, pants down around the [butt] crack. Isn't that a sign of something or are you waiting for Jesus to pull his pants up? Isn't it a sign of something when she's got her dress all the way up to the crack—and got all kinds of [piercings] and things going through her body. What part of Africa did this come from? We are not Africans. Those people are not Africans; they don't know a damned thing about Africa. With names like Shaniqua, Shaligua, Mohammed and all that crap and all of them are in jail. When we give these kinds names to our children, we give them the strength and inspiration in the meaning of those names. What's the point of giving them strong names if there is not parenting and values backing it up.

Brown versus the Board of Education is no longer the white person's problem. We've got to take the neighborhood back.

SOURCE. *"Dr. Bill Cosby Speaks at the 50th Anniversary Commemoration of the* Brown vs. Topeka Board of Education *Supreme Court Decision," speech transcript. Eight Cities Media and Publications, www.eightcitiesmap.com/transcript_bc.htm.*

against: welfare reform, dwindling resources, export of jobs and ongoing racial stigma. And then there are the problems of the working poor: folk who rise up early every day and often work more than forty hours a week, and yet barely, if ever, make it above the poverty level. We must acknowledge the plight of both poor black (single) mothers and poor black fathers, and the lack of social support they confront. Hence, it is incredibly difficult to spend as much time with children as poor black parents might like, especially since they will be demonized if they fail to provide for their children's basic needs. But doing so deflects critical attention and time from child-rearing duties—duties that are difficult enough for two-parent, two-income, intact middle-class families. The characteristics Cosby cites are typical of all families that confront poverty the world over. They are not indigenous to the black poor; they are symptomatic of the predicament of poor people in general. . . .

> The failure of *Brown v. Board* to instigate sufficient change in the nation's schools suggests that the greatest burden—and responsibility—should be on crumbling educational infrastructures.

Resegregation Hurts Poor African Americans

Cosby's views on education have in some respects changed for the worse. His earlier take on the prospects of schooling for the poor was more humane and balanced. In his 1976 dissertation [for his Doctor of Education degree from the University of Massachusetts], Cosby argued against "institutional racism" and maintained that school systems failed the poorest and most vulnerable black students. It is necessary as well to acknowledge the resegregation of American education (when in truth it was hardly desegregated to begin with). The failure of *Brown v. Board* to instigate sufficient change in the nation's schools suggests that the greatest burden—and responsibility—should be on crumbling educational infrastructures. In suburban neighborhoods, there are $60-million schools with state-of-the-art technology, while inner city schools fight desperately for funding for their students. And anti-intellectualism, despite Cosby's claims, is hardly a black phenomenon; it is endemic to the culture. . . . All of this suggests that structural barriers, much more than personal desire, shape the educational experiences of poor blacks. . . .

Cosby's comments don't exist in a cultural or political vacuum. His views have traction in conservative (and

some liberal) circles because they bolster the belief that less money, political action and societal intervention—and more hard work and personal responsibility—are the key to black success. While Cosby can surely afford to ignore what white folk think, the majority of black folk can't reasonably dismiss whites in influential places. Cosby has said that he's not worried about how the white right wing might use his speech, but it certainly fits nicely with their twisted views of the black poor. The poor folk Cosby has hit the hardest are most vulnerable to the decisions of the powerful groups of which he has demanded the least: public policy makers, the business and social elite, and political activists. Poor black folk cannot gain asylum from the potentially negative effects of Cosby's words on public policy makers and politicians

At the *Brown v. Board of Education* 50th Anniversary Gala on May 17, 2004, in Washington, DC, Bill Cosby (center) poses with NAACP president Kweisi Mfume (left) and Howard University president H. Patrick Swygert. **© Stephen Boitano/Getty Images.**

who decide to put into play measures that support Cosby's narrow beliefs.

Cosby also contends that black folk can't blame white folk for our plight. His discounting of structural forces and his exclusive focus on personal responsibility, and black self-help, ignore the persistence of the institutional racism Cosby lamented in his dissertation. To be sure, even when black folk argued for social justice, we never neglected the simultaneous pursuit of personal responsibility and self-help, since that's often the only help we had. In the end, Cosby's views may make white and black liberal fence-sitters unfairly critical of the black poor. Cosby may even convince them that personal behavior will help the poor more than social programs, thus letting white and black elites off the hook. . . .

It is clear that Cosby has touched a raw nerve of class and generation in black America. What he said—and our response to it—goes far beyond a single speech before a group of blacks who were celebrating the achievements of the past. This story is so powerful and controversial, and continues to resonate in our society, because it goes to the heart of the struggle for the identity of a culture. . . .

The conversation that Cosby has started endures because the people who must engage him, and the issues he has raised, are likewise enduring. Thus, what Cosby said reflects on the griefs and hopes and losses and pains of an entire generation of noble men and women who nonetheless, like the rest of us, are human and at times frail and misled. We must learn from each other, listen to each other, correct each other and struggle with each other if the destiny of our people is to be secure. And we must fight for the best that is within our reach, even if that means disagreeing with icons and resisting the myopia of mighty men. What Cosby started is left to us to finish.

VIEWPOINT 9

Brown Has Influenced Human Rights Internationally

Ruth Bader Ginsburg

The following viewpoint comes from a speech delivered by a US Supreme Court justice at the University of Pretoria in South Africa. She explains how legalized segregation in the United States was similar to apartheid and Nazi policies toward non-Aryans and how the 1954 *Brown v. Board of Education* decision affected human rights worldwide. Many around the world hailed the ruling when it was announced, she writes, and the decision helped encourage global change in international human rights. *Brown*'s influence helped efforts for equal rights for women and even of the equal rights within Israel of its Arab citizens, the author states. Ruth Bader Ginsburg is the second woman to be a member of the US Supreme Court, where she has served since 1993.

SOURCE. Ruth Bader Ginsburg, "*Brown v. Board of Education* in International Context," Centre for Human Rights, University of Pretoria, South Africa. February 7, 2006.

Although the *Brown* [*v. Board of Education* (1954 and 1955)] decision did not refer to international law or opinion, there is little doubt that the climate of the era explains, in significant part, why apartheid in America began to unravel in the late 1940s, in the aftermath of World War II. The United States and its allies had fought, successfully, to destroy Hitler's Holocaust Kingdom and the rank racism that prevailed during the years of Nazi ascendancy in Europe. Yet our own troops, when we entered that War, were racially segregated. In the midst of the War, in 1942, Swedish economist Gunnar Myrdal published *The American Dilemma* in which he observed: "America, for its international prestige, power and future security, needs to demonstrate to the world that American Negroes can be satisfactorily integrated into its democracy."

Illustrative of the growing awareness as the War progressed, a young Rabbi, Roland B. Gittelsohn, then a service chaplain, delivered a eulogy over newly-dug graves of U.S. Marines on the Pacific Island of Iwo Jima. In words preserved at the Harry S. Truman Presidential Library, Rabbi Gittelsohn spoke of the way it was, and the way it should be:

> Here lie men who loved America . . . , officers and men, Negroes and whites, rich men and poor, together. . . . Here no man prefers another because of his faith, or despises him because of his color. . . . Among these men there is no discrimination, no prejudice, no hatred. Theirs is the highest and purest democracy. . . . Whoever of us . . . thinks himself superior to those who happen to be in the minority, makes of this ceremony, and of the bloody sacrifice it commemorates, [a] . . . hollow mockery.

> 'The segregation and extermination of non-Aryans in Hitler's Germany were shocking for Americans, but they also served as a troublesome analogy.'

To this, then, as our solemn, sacred duty do we, the living, now dedicate ourselves, to the right of Protestants, Catholics and Jews, of white men and Negroes alike, to enjoy the democracy for which all of them have here paid the price."

The author of the *Brown* decision, Chief Justice Earl Warren, reflected some 18 years after the 1954 judgment:

> The reversal of race relation policies in the United States "was fostered primarily by the presence of [World War II] itself. First, the primary enemy of the Allies, Nazi Germany, was perhaps the most conspicuously and brutally racist nation in the history of the world. . . . The segregation and extermination of non-Aryans in Hitler's Germany were shocking for Americans, but they also served as a troublesome analogy. While proclaiming themselves inexorably opposed to Hitler's practices, many Americans were tolerating the segregation and humiliation of nonwhites within their own borders. The contradiction between the egalitarian rhetoric employed against the Nazis and the presence of racial segregation in America was a painful one."

> 'Racial discrimination . . . raises doubts even among friendly nations as to the intensity of our devotion to the democratic faith.'

The Cold War between the United States and the Soviet Union was in full sway in 1954, the year *Brown v. Board* was decided. University of Virginia Law Professor Michael Klarman, author of a monumental 2004 publication, titled *From Jim Crow to Civil Rights*, wrote of the era: "U.S. democracy was on trial, and southern white supremacy was its greatest vulnerability, made all the more conspicuous by the postwar overthrow of colonial regimes throughout the world." President Truman's civil rights committee cautioned: "[T]he United States is not so strong, the final triumph of the democratic ideal is not so inevitable, that we can ignore what the rest of the world thinks of our record."

In an amicus brief for the United States filed in *Brown*, the Attorney General urged:

> The existence of discrimination against minority groups in the United States has an adverse effect upon our relations with other countries. Racial discrimination . . . raises doubts even among friendly nations as to the intensity of our devotion to the democratic faith.

The brief included a letter from Secretary of State Dean Acheson on the negative impact of race discrimination upon the conduct of U.S. foreign relations. Acheson wrote:

> The United States is under constant attack in the foreign press, over the foreign radio, and in such international bodies as the United Nations because of various practices of discrimination against minority groups in this country. . . . [T]he continuance of racial

Students protest apartheid at a university in Johannesburg, South Africa, in 1989. The *Brown* decision is credited with inspiring change to South Africa's segregated systems. © **Walter Dhaldhla/AFP/Getty Images.**

> discrimination in the United States remains a source of constant embarrassment to this Government in the day-to-day conduct of its foreign relations; and it jeopardizes the effective maintenance of our moral leadership of the free and democratic nations of the world.

Within an hour of the Chief Justice's announcement of the Court's unanimous conclusion that, "[i]n the field of public education, the doctrine of 'separate but equal' has no place," the Voice of America [radio] broadcast the news, in 34 languages, around the globe. The U.S. Information Agency promptly placed articles on *Brown* in almost every African journal. *Time* magazine commented: "In many countries, where U.S. prestige and leadership have been damaged by the fact of U.S. segregation, it will come as a timely reassertion of the basic American principle that 'all men are created equal.'" *Newsweek* magazine observed: "[S]egregation in the public schools has become a symbol of inequality. . . . Now that symbol lies shattered."

The press in Western Europe similarly applauded *Brown*. In Paris, *Le Monde* announced on its front page: "This long-awaited judgment marks a victory of justice over racial prejudice, a victory of democracy. . . ." The *Times* of London hailed the decision as "among the most important and far-reaching [the U.S. Supreme Court] has ever handed down." The *Manchester Guardian* expressed "immense relief" that the United States had "put behind it what has long been its worst reproach. . . ." South of the U.S. border, the Municipal Council in San Paulo, Brazil, cheered *Brown* as "establishing the just equality of the races, essential to universal harmony and peace."

In Africa, coverage was extensive. A dispatch from the American Consul in Dakar, Senegal, reported that the decision was "greeted with enthusiasm in French West Africa although the press [there] has expressed some slight skepticism over its implementation." The weekly

Afrique Nouvelle reported on *Brown* under this headline: "At last! Whites and Blacks in the United States on the same school benches." Black members of Kenya's Legislative Council expressed the hope that their country would follow suit:

> Here in Kenya we are supposed to create one nation of all races. If we are not educated together, we will live in fear of one another. If we are to stay together forever, why should we have separate schools? Children will learn to know each other intimately in the same schools and fear will disappear.

Not all reactions to *Brown* were positive. A dispatch from the U.S. Embassy in South Africa reported: "Most South African Whites are segregationists . . . [T]hough they may see some similarity in America's color problem, [they] regard their own racial situation as having no true parallel elsewhere. Their interest in the decision, then, would be very academic." But just four years later, British Prime Minister Harold Macmillan spoke out in South Africa's Parliament against apartheid. He referred to the "wind of change" blowing through the continent of Africa, change *Brown* helped to promote.

> *Brown* had demonstrated 'the ability of courts to promote human rights and [of] lawyers to effect social change.'

Massive resistance to *Brown* mounted in the South of the United States in the late 1950s continuing into the 1960s. Foreign publications took note. Despite, or perhaps because of, the southern defiance, the world recognized that the U.S. Supreme Court had stepped ahead of the country's political branches (Congress and the President) and prevailing views in many States in pursuit of equal justice under law.

The pursuit of equal justice under law became a major part of the international human rights agenda. In 1965, the United Nations presented for ratification the International Convention on the Elimination of all Forms of Racial Discrimination. Signed by 180 States as of January 2006, and at last ratified by the United States in 1994, the Convention provides that the State Parties "particularly condemn racial segregation and apartheid and undertake to prevent, prohibit and eradicate all practices of this nature in territories under their jurisdiction."

Of the enduring legacy of *Brown*, Richard Goldstone, retired Justice of the South African Constitutional Court, and Brian Ray, Justice Goldstone's 2003 term foreign law clerk, wrote that *Brown* had demonstrated "the ability of courts to promote human rights and [of] lawyers to effect social change." Goldstone and Ray referred to decisions in Canada, South Africa, Trinidad & Tobago citing *Brown* on the importance of education and equal access to it in a democratic society. Those authors also noted cases in New Zealand and South Africa citing *Brown* on the power of courts to "issu[e] orders that would impact budget decisions," orders that might require continuing court surveillance.

On a personal note, *Brown* and its forerunners, along with the movement for international human rights ensued, powerfully influenced the women's rights litigation in the USA in which I was engaged in the 1970s. Thurgood Marshall and his co-workers sought to educate the U.S. Supreme Court, step by step, about the pernicious effects of race discrimination. Similarly, advocates for gender equality sought to inform the Court, through a series of cases, about the injustice of laws ordering or reinforcing separate spheres of human activity for men and women. The ACLU's Women's Rights Project, which I helped to launch and direct, was among the organizations inspired by the NAACP Legal Defense and Education Fund's example.

Advocates of equal citizenship stature for men and women laboring in the 1970s, of course, did not encounter the brand of opposition Thurgood Marshall and his aides experienced in his years at the helm of the NAACP's Legal Defense and Education Fund. Our lives were never in danger because of our advocacy, and we had no problem finding accommodations when we were litigating cases out of town. But of one thing there was no doubt. We gained courage and inspiration from the litigation campaign that led to and followed *Brown*. We copied the strategy of educating judicial audiences in measured movements, in ways digestible by, and palatable to, the decisionmakers. *Brown* figured several years ago in a typically fine decision by Israel's Chief Justice, Aharon Barak. The Israel Land Administration had denied the asserted right of Arabs to build their homes on land in Israel open to the general public for home construction. The Administration defended reservation of permission to build to non-Arab applicants on the promise that it would allocate land to establish an exclusively Arab communal settlement. Citing *Brown*, the Israeli Supreme Court ruled that such allegedly separate-but-equal treatment constituted unlawful discrimination on the basis of national origin.

To sum up, *Brown* both reflected and propelled the development of human rights protection internationally. It was decided with the horrors of the Holocaust in full view, and with the repressive regimes in the Soviet Union, Eastern Europe, and South Africa a then current reality. It propelled an evolution yet unfinished toward respect, in law and in practice, for the human dignity of all the world's people.

VIEWPOINT 10

School Integration in Eastern Europe Contrasts Sharply with the US Experience

Jack Greenberg

In the following viewpoint, one of the lawyers involved in the 1954 US Supreme Court case *Brown v. Board of Education* compares the experiences of integration in eastern Europe in the early twenty-first century with the United States in the 1950s. He writes that he was asked to visit Hungary during its integration of Roma (sometimes called "Gypsy") children into public schools. He witnessed the smooth and peaceful integration of the Roma children and pondered why the experience of African Americans in US schools was so different. After thoughtful consideration, he concludes that the ideology behind integration was already understood and popular in eastern Europe before schools were integrated. He also writes that the understanding of racial integration around the world and in Europe was made

---

SOURCE. Jack Greenberg, "Remarks of Jack Greenberg," *St. John's Law Review*, vol. 78, no. 2, Spring 2004. Reproduced by permission.

possible in part, and greatly influenced by, *Brown*. Attorney and legal scholar Jack Greenberg was the only white legal counselor for the Legal Defense and Educational Fund (LDF) of the National Association for the Advancement of Colored People (NAACP). In 1961 he succeeded Thurgood Marshall as director of the LDF.

Earlier this year, I visited Budapest and Sofia in connection with Roma-integration programs in Eastern Europe designed affirmatively to integrate Roma children, also known as Gypsies, into public schools in Eastern Europe. I was invited to participate in this work because of my experience with *Brown* [*v. Board of Education* (1954 and 1955)] and school desegregation in the United States. The only analogy for my experience is that when you learn a foreign language you understand English better. When I participated in the integration of the Roma into public schools of Eastern Europe, I gained a better understanding of what happened here immediately following the *Brown* decision and in its aftermath.

In 2002, the integration had begun with 2,400 Roma children being introduced into public schools in six towns in Bulgaria. When I visited those schools and saw how the integration was going, I was amazed and thunderstruck because the beginning of the integration was smooth. It was successful and it was greeted by community goodwill. It was everything anybody could have hoped for; its contrast to what occurred in the United States in 1954 could not have been greater.

Photo on following page: A teacher leads a class with Roma children in Romania. The *Brown v. Board of Education* experience in the United States influenced school integration in Eastern Europe. © **J.W. Alker/imageBROKER/Alamy.**

When *Brown* was decided in the United States, the effect of the decision neared a revolution in the South. The 101 southern congressmen and senators adopted the Southern Manifesto, in which they denounced the Supreme Court of the United States. "Impeach Earl Warren" campaigns proliferated throughout the country. The southern states set up state sovereignty commissions. They passed statutes requiring that public schools be

Popularii și optimații
Plebeii
au cerut drepturi
legi scrise
Tiberius și Caius Gracchus
133 î.H. Tiberius propune legi

closed if they were integrated. They passed other statutes setting up impenetrable barriers to integration. There was persecution of civil rights groups—Alabama for example banned the NAACP from functioning in the state. Civil rights lawyers were the subject of disbarment proceedings all over the South. We all remember Little Rock. In towns where integration had been attempted or begun, the National Guard, state police, and sometimes federal troops were frequently called out.

In Eastern Europe, school desegregation proceeded smoothly.

Integration in Eastern Europe

Nothing could have contrasted more with what occurred in Eastern Europe. **In Eastern Europe, school desegregation proceeded smoothly.** Fifty years after *Brown*, with very little happening on the integration front, I began to ponder the situation. It occurred to me that Eastern Europe is politically hospitable to the idea of integrating schools while the South was not. One reason why Eastern Europe has been receptive to integration is that entry into the European Union is conditioned upon integration. Thus, Bulgaria, Hungary, Czechoslovakia, and Slovakia must integrate their public schools in order to be admitted into the European Union. In an effort to comply, Bulgaria, Hungary, and other Eastern European states have passed national statutes that require integration. Similarly, Hungary has passed a framework program recognizing the need for integration.

When Bulgarian public schools integrated the 2,400 Roma children into the formerly non-Roma schools, those schools benefited from supportive social programs. Social workers visited every single home in the community. Schools furnished tutors for children and the communities provided meals and clothing to those children who were most in need. Cultural programs took place in which Roma and Bulgarian children interacted. I attended a meeting in one school of about three-hundred students, where students, administrators, teachers—Roma and non-Roma—all praised what had occurred and boasted of the fact that the second-highest scoring student on the national math exam was a Roma child who had been integrated into the public school. It then occurred to me that school integration in the United States did not begin to be successful to the extent it even has been-until the United States reached a stage in which the politics and the public receptivity was at the same level as it currently is in Eastern Europe.

"I then understood that *Brown* had a dual role. . . . It acted like an icebreaker that . . . changed the politics of the country."

Understanding *Brown*'s Role in the United States

I then understood that *Brown* had a dual role. It provided for integration of schools, but *Brown* also had another role. It acted like an icebreaker that crashed through a frozen sea and changed the politics of the country. Until *Brown*, senators by the names of Eastland, Talmadge, Russell, and others dominated the politics of the South, indeed of the entire country. They controlled what was happening in the South and they also exercised considerable influence in the North. For example, Senator Stennis once refused to bring a military appropriations bill before the Senate unless President Nixon intervened with the United States Court of Appeals for the Fifth Circuit, by asking the court to recall some school desegregation orders issued at the time. The President intervened; the Fifth Circuit listened to him. I brought the case before the United States Supreme Court and it reversed the Fifth Circuit's decision. *Brown* rebuffed the dominant powers that existed.

Brown then gave rise to the civil rights movement's sit-ins and Freedom Rides. Those who doubt that *Brown* succeeded in creating those changes need only remember the sit-ins. Sit-in demonstrators said *Brown* inspired them. The first Freedom Ride ended in New Orleans on May 17, 1961, which is the anniversary of *Brown*. Martin Luther King held prayer pilgrimages. *Brown* also inspired and helped bring about the Civil Rights Acts of 1964, 1965, and 1968, which led to significant political changes. Now we have many black congressmen; the mayor of every large and most small cities in the United States is, or has been, black at one time. A complete change has taken place.

While it is always a mistake to look at some particular factor in history and attribute everything to it, you certainly can say that *Brown* played a major part in the civil rights movement. As that transition occurred, the United States approached issues of race and school desegregation in a way that Eastern Europe would later approach the integration of the Roma. Integration of the Roma came out of parallel developments in Eastern Europe, such as the Holocaust, which greatly injured Jews as well as the Romas; the Universal Declaration of Human Rights; the European Convention on Human Rights; the establishment of the European Court of Human Rights; and the pervasive influence of human rights ideology throughout Eastern Europe. All of these events occurred following World War II and now culminate in the requirements placed on Eastern European countries by the European Union.

The United States did not begin to reach integration until the mid-1960s. Because of my experiences with desegregation in the United States and Eastern Europe, I perceive *Brown* as not only a school desegregation case, but also as a case that changed the country's politics in a way that made integration of the schools possible and opened new arenas to integration.

CHAPTER 3

Personal Narratives

VIEWPOINT 1

School Life for an African American Boy Before Desegregation

William E. Cox

In the following viewpoint, a publishing executive recounts his firsthand experience of "separate but equal" schools before the 1954 *Brown v. Board of Education* ruling. He describes the conditions in his segregated school in Alabama as well as the role of his praiseworthy teachers and administrators. He and his young classmates were completely unaware of how different their school was from white schools. Despite their many limitations, he and many others like him valued education and went on to higher education and successful careers. William E. Cox is the president and cofounder of a publishing services company and the president and managing editor of *Black Issues in Higher Education*.

Photo on previous page: Students at the all-black Thomy Lafon School in New Orleans gather at a window in 1954. **© Robert W. Kelley/Time Life Pictures/ Getty Images.**

SOURCE. William E. Cox, "Reflections of One Who Was There," *The Unfinished Agenda of Brown v. Board of Education,* Editors of Black Issues in Higher Education with James Anderson and Dara N. Burne, eds. Hoboken, NJ: John Wiley and Sons, 2004, pp. xvi–xxi.

I look at the *Brown v. Board of Education* decision by the Supreme Court of the United States in 1954 through a different lens from most Americans. My perspective may not even be shared by the majority of African Americans who have felt the beneficial impact of *Brown* over the past half century, because I am a black man who was born, raised, educated, and had my career roots in the Deep South during the era of "separate but equal," a phenomenon that can be best described as a hoax.

I experienced segregation first hand. It was not something my elders shared with me—not something I read about in a novel or a history book. I lived segregation. Mention segregated lunch counters, water fountains, restrooms, and schools and I can take you there. My memories of those experiences are as vivid and poignant as if they happened yesterday.

Experiencing Jim Crow First Hand

Life in Bay Minette, Alabama, in post-World War II America was very much like life in other parts of the Deep South. Even though the war between the North and the South had ended some eighty years before, the segregation of people by the color of their skin was still the prevailing custom of the times.

Signs that directed "colored" to another entrance to a restaurant (often a take-out window in the rear) or bathroom is a vivid memory to me. I saw these signs in my community and everywhere I was willing to travel in my boyhood and adolescence. I say willing to travel, because blacks in the Deep South knew they were taking certain risks each time they ventured beyond both the visible and invisible borders that had been placed there by those wanting to separate the races.

When I started school in 1948, my first year was spent in a two-room building, Pine Grove Grammar School, in Bay Minette, that held twenty students. Segregated for

> Little if any care ever went into [the school building's] maintenance. A paintbrush probably had never touched the structure.

the many years that it existed, that building housed six grades taught by two teachers—three grades each. That building is etched in my memory. Little if any care ever went into its maintenance. A paintbrush probably had never touched the structure. But it was the very first place I called school. I thought my first-grade teacher, Miss Kisiah V. Autry, was the smartest person in the world. In fact, she did not even have a college degree but had achieved about as much education as blacks could achieve in those days of crushing oppression. Miss Autry continued to pursue her studies each summer and eventually obtained her baccalaureate degree and met the certification standards set by the state of Alabama for teachers. The second person who had a significant educational impact on my life was Mrs. Nellie Lee Elmore, who had served as the teacher/supervisor of that small school for black children in Baldwin County; some would say that her position was the equivalent of superintendent of schools. I mention this about her title and responsibilities because, after the closing of Pine Grove Grammar School, she was not allowed to perform administrative duties or assume an educational leadership role in the white school system. Like so many black educational leaders of her day, she was assigned classroom-teaching duties in an elementary school when the changes resulting from *Brown* slowly began to take effect.

Limitations—and Possibilities—in Segregated Schools

The black students attending segregated schools had few clues as to how different their education was from that of the white children going to school down the road a few miles. I didn't know that my textbooks were the used textbooks of others, that our science and athletic equipment represented the hand-me-downs of the other schools in the district.

I attended that small grammar school for one year before it closed. I went on to a larger school—Douglasville High School. Still segregated, it was a larger facility serving a broader community of black students. Our two teachers joined a much larger faculty. Twenty students now joined approximately three hundred. But most of my educational experiences remained inferior to those being enjoyed by white students in the community, the state of Alabama, and the nation.

My classmates and I had limited opportunities and challenging boundaries that restricted us from moving too far away from our homes and families. Few black youth of the 1950s and early 1960s in Alabama or other places in the Deep South could expect to see their education going much beyond a high school diploma. And many didn't even achieve that milestone. My classmates and I struggled to succeed and received little attention for our special needs. Those who succeeded in attaining a diploma had few paths to follow upon graduating. My sole first-grade classmate at Pine Grove Grammar School became pregnant and dropped out in her teens—a path repeated by far too many young women of the time. Unemployment or underemployment was far more prevalent than postsecondary education and career opportunities.

> Few of us knew then about the incredible world of educational and career opportunities that existed beyond our immediate world.

I didn't comprehend that our teachers—as committed, energetic, and caring as they were—were measured by a different yardstick of professional preparation. It never dawned on me that per-pupil expenditures for black students in Bay Minette were only a small percentage of that spent for whites. Because of the boundaries that restricted so many young blacks, few of us knew then about the incredible world of educational and career opportunities that existed beyond our immediate world.

A Legacy of Individual High Accomplishment

Those less than ideal conditions did not hinder a significant number of individuals from achieving in school and continuing on to success in a myriad of career endeavors. Their individual accomplishments are a testament to the power of the person and his will to succeed. They met the challenges brought on by the inequities of segregation and made the most of the educational experiences afforded them.

Included among my student associates at Douglasville High School was Henry Sanders, who went on to acquire a law degree from Harvard University and is serving with distinction in the Senate of the state of Alabama. Clarence Gardner earned a Ph.D in engineering and enjoyed a successful career as a U.S. Air Force officer. John Carter became a successful high school principal in Camden, Alabama, while Janice Anderson Inge and Eloise Watson Gardner committed their lives and careers to teaching in the school systems of Los Angeles, California, and Mobile, Alabama, respectively.

The city of Baton Rouge, Louisiana, benefited from the talents of Jerald Boykin, an alumnus who went on to become assistant to the mayor and director of personnel for Louisiana's capital city. And Mattie Harris Hardy brought honor to students attending Faulkner State College, where she served as a student services professional. Many of my peers are serving as ministers, health care professionals, and entrepreneurs in towns and cities across Alabama and the nation. Their common denominator was that they rose from a segregated education in the United States and made the most of their futures in the worlds of business, military, government, education, and an array of different settings.

Home and Family Life

Life away from school embodied experiences that I'm certain I shared with many of my peers. My father, Jesee Cox, died when I was ten years old and I was raised by a very loving, hardworking mother. A deeply religious woman, Artensie Cox provided for us through her maid service to white families in the Bay Minette community, pursuits that she continued until age eighty-two.

My mother was not an educated woman in the "book sense," but she possessed a work ethic and value system that gave solid direction to my three siblings and me. We knew we were loved, and we were taught the meaning of right and wrong. My mother, through what we would today call "parenting skills," taught me self-reliance—that what I was going to achieve, I was going to have to work very hard for. She believed that a good education was the route to a good career and a better life. She introduced me to values that were reinforced by the strong educators with whom I had the good fortune to study, in school and later in college. She was not financially able to send me to college, but she helped. I had to work for 3½ of my college years, until graduation.

> "I understood that if I wanted more out of life, education was the way to achieve it."

While the specific opportunities being denied to black students were unknown to me at the time, the boundaries were eminently clear. From my mother, I learned about the borders that existed in the segregated South and the dangers associated with getting too close or to crossing them. I learned where to travel and what behaviors to display in which environments. The geographic boundaries were the easy ones. I knew what section of Bay Minette I could be in at what time of the day and night. I also learned the consequences a young black man could face if he violated those boundaries.

Learning the Value of Higher Education

From my life experiences, my family, and those educators, I understood that if I wanted more out of life, education was the way to achieve it. I developed fairly lofty goals for a young man whose life experiences sheltered me from educational and career potential and hid from me effective expression of the gifts I possessed.

Alabama A&M, a historically black college in Huntsville, Alabama, was to eventually play an important role in my life. The "college on the hill" became for me what other historically black colleges and universities are to so many black Americans—a stepping-stone to the future.

I had never been on a college campus until the day I went to A&M for the first time. There was a sense of promise—of opportunity—that I recognized that first day. I knew if my life were to be different, education was going to play a major part in that change, and I "took" to college immediately. College was to be a major factor in my life.

The Sister of a *Brown* Plaintiff Remembers Student Strikes for Better School Conditions

Joan Johns Cobb

The following viewpoint tells the story of how Barbara Rose Johns came to lead her classmates in a strike to protest the conditions at their substandard school in Virginia. Her efforts included recruiting NAACP lawyers to help them bring a lawsuit—one of the similar cases that would be joined into *Brown v. Board of Education* (1954) when it was heard by the US Supreme Court. The school, Robert Russa Moton High School, is now a historic landmark and civil rights museum. Johns died in 1991. Her heroic story is told by Joan Johns Cobb, her younger sister.

In 1951 my family was living in Arlington Heights, Virginia, which is in Prince Edward County, on a farm. My father was a farmer. My mother worked

---

SOURCE. Joan Johns Cobb, "Eyewitness to Jim Crow: Joan John Cobb Remembers," CORE.org. Reproduced by permission.

in Washington, D.C., during the week at the U.S. Navy Department. She would travel home on weekends. There were five children in the family—two girls and one boy. My sister, Barbara, was the eldest. I have three brothers: Ernest, Roderick and Robert.

In 1951 I was a freshman in high school. My three brothers were in elementary school at the time. My sister, Barbara, was a junior. The school I attended was Robert R. Moton High School in Farmville, Virginia. The school was for black students only. There was a white school in Farmville. I believe the name of it was Prince Edward School. We had separate facilities and most of the school supplies that we got were torn and tattered, and we didn't have enough supplies to write with.

> [To ease school overcrowding] the county decided to build three tarpaper shacks . . . similar to a chicken coop on a farm.

The school we went to was overcrowded. Consequently, **the county decided to build three tarpaper shacks for us to hold classes in.** A tarpaper shack looks like a dilapidated black building, which is similar to a chicken coop on a farm. It's very unsightly. In winter the school was very cold. And a lot of times we had to put on our jackets. Now, the students that sat closest to the wood stove were very warm and the ones who sat farthest away were very cold. And I remember being cold a lot of times and sitting in the classroom with my jacket on. When it rained, we would get water through the ceiling. So there were lots of pails sitting around the classroom. And sometimes we had to raise our umbrellas to keep the water off our heads. It was a very difficult setting for trying to learn.

Doing "Something About It"

And I remember we were always talking about how bad the conditions were but we didn't know what to do about it. So one day my sister and a group of students that she chose decided to do something about it.

My sister was sort of an introvert and she stayed to herself a lot. She was very studious, always reading books and going to the woods to, I guess, meditate. She never told me anything. And afterwards, I questioned her and asked her why she didn't mention it. And she said it was because she couldn't afford to tell anyone because it may have gotten out and it had to be a secret.

There was a music teacher by the name of Inez Davenport that Barbara confided in. When she discussed the conditions of the school with Miss Davenport, Miss Davenport said to her, finally, "Why don't you do something about it?" With that statement, Barbara said she decided to think about that. She tried to come up with a plan of what she could do to get a better school. And she decided to consult with the other four students. Between them they came up with the plan for the school strike.

The first experience that I had that there was something about to happen was when we were called to the assembly in school that day. We had these curtains on the stage that could open up when someone was going to come out for an assembly. That day, when the curtains opened it was my sister on stage rather than the principal. I was totally shocked. She walked up to the podium and she started to tell everyone about the fact that she wanted us to cooperate with her because the school was going out on a strike. I remember sitting in my seat and trying to go as low in the seat as I possibly could because I was so shocked and so upset. I actually was frightened because I knew that what she was doing was going to have severe consequences. I didn't know what they were going to be but I knew there were going to be some. She stood up there and addressed the school. She seemed to have everyone's attention. . . . At one point, she took off her shoe and she banged on the podium and said that we were going to go out on strike and would everyone please

Joan Johns Cobb greets Virginia governor Bob McDonnell at the unveiling of a portrait of her sister, civil rights activist Barbara Johns, in the state capitol in 2010. **© AP Photo/Richmond TimesDispatch/Bob Brown.**

cooperate and "don't be afraid, just follow us out." So we did. The entire student body followed her out.

They had devised a plan for the principal to be away from the school at the moment. So one of the students—I believe it was John Watson—called from downtown to say that some of the students were hanging around downtown. So he [the principal] got in his car and drove down there to get the students and that's when she [Barbara] called the assembly and asked all the teachers to leave. They reluctantly left, all except one. I think one was a little persistent about staying but I believe that teacher eventually left too.

We walked out to the school grounds and awaited further instructions. Then later we were just loaded on the buses and went home, as usual. But I do remember being shocked and frightened . . . not knowing what was going to happen next. Because I knew that you did not do anything in the community to upset the white establishment. And I knew something very bad was going to happen as a result of it. . . . It was April 23, 1951.

Getting the NAACP Involved

Over the next few days that we were home there was a lot of activity going on as far as meetings were concerned because we [the black student body] met at the First Baptist Church in Farmville, Virginia. Reverend [Leslie] Griffin was the pastor at that time. . . . I think Reverend Griffin advised that the NAACP had to become involved in it. And somewhere along the way my sister decided to call Spotswood Robinson and Oliver Hill in Richmond, Virginia, to see if they could help us.

> [Attorney] Oliver Hill . . . said [Barbara] just kept calling him until he decided to take the case.

Spotswood Robinson and Oliver Hill were lawyers. . . . It was my understanding that Mr. Robinson at first did not respond to the call because he was busy and so was Oliver Hill . . . they didn't have the time to come to Farmville to see what was going on. However, Mr. Oliver Hill would tell me later that he got a call from Barbara and she was very persistent. She told him that we needed him and that he just had to come. . . . He said that she said to him, "You must come and help us." He said she just kept calling him until he decided to take the case.

The Real Threat of Violence

We [the black community] were a separate entity. We were the black students and the black children. We had no interaction except for when you went to the supermarket or the department stores. Occasionally we had interaction on the farm in that some of our black fathers

People were afraid of lynchings. That was the thing that was foremost in everyone's mind.

would work for the white farmers. And other than that, and seeing them in stores, we had no communication.

I do remember that we had a cross burned at the school.

My grandmother and some of the other family members [were] not able to go to the local stores and charge goods or food or whatever they had been doing before. . . . And I remember my uncle telling me, who was in the logging business, that he suffered too because they wouldn't allow him to have credit. So it was a financial strain on the black community after that happened. We were able to get credit for clothes and food at different times and that was all taken away.

People were afraid of lynchings. That was the thing that was foremost in everyone's mind. Because at the time, you still read of lynchings and you heard about lynchings. And so therefore, everyone was afraid that he or she would be lynched. Even, at the time, for talking back to a white person or in the case of the black men, speaking to a white woman. So we all lived with that type of fear. It was real. It was scary.

One weekend [in 1954] we traveled to Washington, D.C., to visit one of my relatives, my aunt. And when we came back—actually before we got home—my uncle called up my aunt's house to tell us that our house was burning. And when we got back, we saw our house in flames—in ashes really. And to this day, we don't know what happened to our house. . . . I remember we had to live with my grandmother . . . during my senior year in high school. . . . Then in 1955 we moved to Washington, D.C. That's where we stayed up until the time I got married and moved to New Jersey. I believe [my parents] decided to move because of jobs because at that time their financial situation was very critical. Because my father was farmer it was hard after the strike for him to get credit.

Barbara left the county in 1951. She went with my uncle Vernon Johns to live in Montgomery, Alabama. My parents decided that it was not a safe place for her to be for the school year coming up. . . .

> I don't believe Barbara knew anything about the fact that [her walkout] would change the course of history.

Changing History

I don't believe Barbara knew anything about the fact that this [her walk-out] would change the course of history. However, I remember her being so excited and shouting about it when the decision came down and we heard about it. . . . I don't think she knew that what she and the other students did would have any kind of impact on the nation that resulted in the *Brown v. Board of Education* case. . . .

I feel very proud of the fact that my sister and the other students took a stand and decided to do something about getting a new school. I am happy that the decision they made happened to be part of the *Brown v. Board of Education* decision of 1954. I think it was wonderful and almost unbelievable that they played a role in bringing about that case. I'm very proud of that. I'm very proud of the role my sister played in all of this. I'm just beginning to really appreciate how important it was and what a great thing she did at the age of 16. When I think about it now, it's just awesome. I can hardly believe it happened. Whereas I was a freshman then, I don't feel I had any real role except to follow instructions. So I guess you may say we all are a part of history. I give all the credit to my sister and the fellow students that planned the strike and really carried it out. It's incredible.

VIEWPOINT 3

A Lawyer Representing Kansas Recalls His Supreme Court Argument

Paul E. Wilson

In the following viewpoint, a lawyer tells his story of defending the Kansas school segregation laws at the US Supreme Court. In his mind, the law was clear, and the state was not in violation of it. The theory he presented to the Supreme Court hinged on whether "separate but equal" was still to be followed. He attempted to persuade the court that the issue of whether segregated schools had a detrimental effect on children was not relevant to the case. He remembers listening to the opposition lawyers present the case against segregation and how their oratorical style was more forceful and eloquent than his own. He writes that the justices seemed to listen to his adversaries

---

SOURCE. Paul E. Wilson, "In the Supreme Court: Argument," *A Time to Lose: Representing Kansas in* Brown v. Board of Education. Lawrence: University Press of Kansas, 1995, pp. 142–152.

with deference. During the trial, the author realized he was witnessing the maturing of the American social conscience. Paul E. Wilson served as a county attorney and assistant attorney general in Kansas. He taught at the University of Kansas School of Law and also served on the Kansas Judicial Council. He died in 2001.

By high noon the Court Chamber was filled to its capacity. Officers of the Court, lawyers, litigants, members of their families, and spectators conversed in subdued voices while they awaited the opening of the session. In the Great Hall outside the courtroom several hundred people stood in lines, hopefully awaiting a place in the chamber or at least a glimpse of the Court. Then things began to happen. The marshal's gavel fell, the people in the chamber stood, and three justices emerged through each of three openings in the velvet backdrop as the marshal intoned, "The Honorable, the Chief Justice and the Associate Justices of the Supreme Court of the United States." While the justices moved to their places at the bench, the marshal continued, "Oyez! Oyez! Oyez! All persons having business before the Honorable, the Supreme Court of the United States, are admonished to draw near and give their attention, for the court is now sitting. God save the United States and this Honorable Court." The marshal's gavel again rapped, and those in the courtroom resumed their seats. The Court was in session. . . .

> 'This case resolves itself simply to this: whether the "separate but equal" doctrine is still the law.'

My time had come. The chief justice nodded in my direction and said, "General Wilson." I rose, stood behind the lectern, and, somewhat to my surprise, heard my voice saying, "May it please the Court . . ." Quickly, I tried to emphasize that I appeared only for the state of Kansas and only to defend the constitutionality of a statute passed by the Kansas legislature. I did not represent and carried no brief for the Topeka Board of Education. . . .

Richard Kluger read the transcript of the arguments twenty years after the fact. He found my presentation to be "a perfectly able but somewhat simplistic argument for the state of Kansas." I do not quarrel with the historian's evaluation. I regarded *Brown* as a simple case. The law was, to me, clear and was on our side. The factual justification for the law was more difficult. Hence, I chose to limit my argument to the law. Moreover, in the twenty-odd years that had elapsed between the argument and Kluger's comment, the law governing interracial equality and discrimination had grown vastly more complex. What seemed simplistic in 1972 might have been less so twenty years earlier.

Delivering Kansas' Legal Argument

Since my purpose was to inform the Court, I outlined the statutory scheme of public schools in Kansas, emphasizing that racially segregated elementary schools were permitted, not required, in only a few communities and that in those communities the local policy was for local determination. Also emphasizing the finding of no substantial inequality among the Topeka schools, I suggested that "it is our theory that this case resolves itself simply to this: whether the 'separate but equal' doctrine is still the law, and whether it is to be followed in this case by this Court." At this point, questions from the bench required that I depart from my planned argument. Justice Frankfurter wanted to know how many blacks lived in Kansas (about 73,000 or 4 percent of the total population) and where they lived (more than two-thirds in the twelve cities of the first class). Justice Black asked where Indians went to school (then attended white schools). Justice Frankfurter returned to the act to inquire about the possible consequences of reversal. What problems did I foresee? What further action by the Supreme Court might be needed to carry out the decree? I replied: "In perfect candor, I must say to the Court that the consequences would probably not be serious."

"As I pointed out, our Negro population is small. We do have in our Negro schools Negro teachers, Negro administrators, that would necessarily be assimilated in the school system at large. That might produce some administrative difficulties. I can imagine no serious difficulty beyond that."

Justice Reed asked whether efforts had been made to repeal the statute being challenged in this case. (I knew of none.)

Justice Jackson's turn was next. Of the nine members of the Court, I think I admired Jackson most. He was handsome and dignified, yet relaxed and disarming. He had a human quality not readily discernible in some of his colleagues. I was not uncomfortable when he questioned me. It went like this:

> Justice Jackson: Mr. Attorney General, you emphasized the four percent, and the smallness of the population. Would that affect your problem if there were heavier concentrations?
>
> Mr. Wilson: It is most difficult for me to answer that question. It might. I am not acquainted with the situation where there is a heavier concentration, in other words.
>
> Justice Jackson: I mean, your statute adapts itself to different localities. What are the variables that the statute was designed to take care of, if any, if you now, at this late date?

My response, although unartfully expressed, was intended to convey my belief that considerations of demography, economics, history, and tradition all had an impact on the local decision. . . .

After disposing of these unplanned for and incidental inquiries, I continued with my prepared argument. Emphasizing the opinions of the Kansas Supreme Court on which Kansans had relied, I stressed *Reynolds v. Board of Education of Topeka*. Where, in 1903, the court had faced squarely and found in favor of the constitutionality of the Kansas statute under attack. I continued: . . .

> We think the question before this Court is simply this: Is the *Plessy* case and the *Gong Lum* case and the "separate but equal" doctrine still the law of this land?
>
> We think if you decide in favor of these appellants, the Court will necessarily overrule the doctrines expressed in those cases and, at the same time, will say that the legislatures of the seventeen or twenty-one states, that the Congress of the United States, that dozens of appellate courts have been wrong for a period of more than seventy-five years, when they have believed and have manifested a belief that facilities equal though separate were within the meaning of the Fourteenth Amendment.

The assertion that a reversal would imply that the earlier decisions were wrong aroused objection:

> Justice Burton: Don't you recognize it as possible that within seventy-five years the social and economic conditions and the personal relations of the nation may have changed so that what may have been a valid interpretation of them seventy-five years ago would not be a valid interpretation of the constitutionally today?
>
> Mr. Wilson: We recognize that as a possibility. We do not believe that this record discloses any such change. . . .

That final segment of my presentation was directed at the trial court's Finding of Fact No. 8, which I feared might be our Achilles heel. If the finding were to be accepted as true, if segregation of white and black children does, in fact, have a detrimental effect on the black children, if it retards their educational and mental development and deprives them of benefits they would receive in a racially integrated school system, then it becomes difficult to argue that separate schools are or can be equal. My task therefore, was to persuade the Supreme Court that the finding was not material to the issues before the trial court. . . .

During the last several minutes of my argument the justices asked no questions. They appeared to listen but I suspected that their interest was waning. I had said all that I could honestly say on behalf of Kansas. I doubted that more words would add quality to my argument. To continue would be to invite questions that I might not be able to answer. Although I had used hardly half of my allotted hour, I decided it was time to stop. I sat down. The task that I had anticipated with dread and distress had not been unpleasant. . . .

> "The force and eloquence with which [the ideas about integration] were expressed gave them new vigor and meaning."

Listening to the Opposing Counsel

As John W. Davis moved into the chair that I had vacated, Thurgood Marshall approached the lectern and began to speak. The main event was under way. A dispassionate analyst would find little in the speeches that was new and different. The ideas were ones that I had heard, read or thought of before, but **the force and eloquence with which they were expressed gave them new vigor and meaning.** The contrasting personalities of the adversaries added drama to the debate. Each seemed to be an eminently suitable protagonist of the view that he urged. Mr. Davis, the near octogenarian, was a patrician. His voice was mellow yet strong, his sentences clear

I was satisfied that I had been witness to something special.

and complete, his diction exquisite. The justices listened to his argument with almost deferential respect. Only twice was he interrupted by questions from the bench. He spoke to support an understanding of the Constitution that he believed was rational and just and consistent with traditional American values. His challenger, Thurgood Marshall, was, at forty-five, in the prime years of a brilliant career in advocacy. The descendants of slave and son of a country club steward, he was the product of Baltimore's segregated public school system and of the law school at Washington's then all-Negro Howard University. It is part of the Marshall folklore that as a law student he regularly cut classes to attend Supreme Court sessions whenever John W. Davis was appearing there. He was more laid back than dignified, his speech was more forceful than elegant, and he was more concerned with issues of social justice than with history and precedent. He thought America could do better. Much of his argument emerged in impromptu responses to questions from the bench.

After Davis and Marshall had spoken, I felt that whatever would follow would be superfluous. They had said it all. **I was satisfied that I had been witness to something special**, something that historians would write about for a long time. In the Davis involvement I sensed an element of poignancy—one of the century's greatest advocates employing his wit and eloquence to support a cause that had already been lost, not to Thurgood Marshall and his associates, but to history and the maturing American social conscience.

An NAACP Lawyer Discusses *Brown* and Its Legacy

Jack Greenberg and Gilbert Holmes, interviewed by M. Dion Thompson

The following viewpoint is a part of an interview conducted by *Baltimore Sun* reporter M. Dion Thompson in commemoration of the fiftieth anniversary of *Brown v. Board of Education* (1954). The conversation includes Jack Greenberg, one of the lawyers for the National Association for the Advancement of Colored People (NAACP) who participated in *Brown* at the US Supreme Court, and Gilbert Holmes, a professor of law at the University of Baltimore. In the interview, Greenberg argues that *Brown* was the catalyst for the civil rights movement. He also explains the thinking behind bringing the legal cases demanding school integration. He explains that they could not have predicted the Civil Rights Act of 1964 and expected segregation would happen very gradually. He also recounts the resistance to school integration and some of the violence that resulted from it. The

---

SOURCE. "Interview with Jack Greenberg and Gilbert Holmes," *Baltimore Sun*, May 18, 2004. Reproduced by permission.

participants also discuss how schools and communities have become more segregated in recent years, and future challenges will revolve around employment and economic opportunity.

Jack Greenberg: *Brown* was filed as a case to integrate schools, and for a long while it didn't do that simply because of massive resistance. You had about a hundred congressman and senators denouncing the Supreme Court, and all kinds of other resistance. You had violence. There were economic sanctions against people . . . Then it went into decline . . . I don't think anybody thought it would follow that trajectory. But at the same time a great many things happened that we had not foreseen.

Brown was a catalyst for the creation of the Civil Rights movement. It didn't do it all by itself, but there's no better evidence of that than (that) the first Freedom Ride was scheduled to end in New Orleans on May 17. The Freedom Riders were essentially paying homage to *Brown*. And you talk to Civil Rights demonstrators and, yeah, they had *Brown* in mind. Rosa Parks was an official of the NAACP and they drank and breathed *Brown*. But more important, the Montgomery bus boycott came to a successful conclusion when the Legal Defense Fund, our office, filed a law suit to enjoin the enforcement of the Montgomery segregation laws. We won that case. And the entire Supreme Court opinion consisted of quote, *Brown vs. Board of Education*, unquote.

"*Brown* was the catalyst to the Civil Rights Movement, and out of the movement came the Civil Rights Act, which changed everything."

Brown was the catalyst to the Civil Rights Movement, and out of the movement came the Civil Rights Act, which changed everything. Public accommodations integrated almost immediately. Voting took a little longer.

But we went from a situation where black voting in the South, in the areas where black population was greatest, was 2 percent to 8 percent, and now we have 39 black congressmen and the mayor of many a large city is black. So, it would be crazy to say *Brown* did it, but on the other hand, it wouldn't have happened without *Brown*. People who disagree with that are always going to disagree.

A Full Appreciation of *Brown*'s Meaning

I always view *Brown* as a school case, and I also view it as a catalyst to the Movement, the Civil Rights Act and so forth. But I never really had a full appreciation for what it meant to American social politics until last year, last summer, when I went to Eastern Europe and participated in a discussion of the integration of Roma gypsies into the public schools in Eastern Europe. They were highly segregated. I was just so astonished. I went to Bulgaria to see what was happening in terms of the integration of schools.

The cases that led up to *Brown* came out of a campaign that was led by Charles Houston, based on a study that he had been done by Nathan Margold. And, the Margold Report considered this very question and this was in the late 1920s, the early 30s: Should we go to equalize schools, or should we go to integrate? And he did a study of what would happen.

The law was separate but equal, and what he found to no surprise is that it was not equal, it was not even remotely approaching equal.

And, so Houston considered: Should we file some cases to equalize the schools? He didn't have to file a case to establish the principle that they should be equal, because the principle was there. You had to file cases to really make them do it. And he said, 'Well, we have enough money to file about seven cases, maybe not enough money to file 70 cases.' And he said maybe we would win a lot of them, but then would be the problem of actually wringing the money out of the school districts. The court does not print money. You've got to get it from the legislature. And he thought you would have a hard time doing that. Well, that was an absolutely valid perception.

The next point is, even if you did get the funding, that is not what black kids need. To go to school in a segregated environment is, sometimes, maybe unavoidable. Now, in particular because of residential segregation, it is widely unavoidable, but all the evidence shows that an integrated education is superior to a segregated one, the grades and the scores, but even more than that, the social networking that comes out of an integrated education.

That is not to say you can't have an absolutely first-rate all-black school. There are a few such examples, but I think the term people use is 'can you bring that to scale?' Is that something you can have as a nationwide thing? In a particular school with highly dedicated teachers, those aren't aberrations, but can you sustain that on a national basis?

Achieving Integration in Schools

M. Dion Thompson: You mention earlier that one thing you all were surprised at was the arc of integration, where you have zero, then you have a peak in the early '80s, then tailing back off. Surprised because you thought it would be a continual upswing.

Mr. Greenberg: Well, I want to tell you, we were like, five lawyers, with maybe a couple dozen people we worked with on an ad hoc basis. We weren't sitting around trying to predict the future. We were doing the best we can with the circumstances. So, if somebody said to one of us at that time, what do you think is going to happen? Nobody anticipated the Civil Rights Act would be passed. Nobody anticipated then there would be Title VI. If somebody said, 'What do you think will happen?' I would have said: The same thing would happen that happened on

Jack Greenberg participates in a planning meeting in 1965, when he was the director of the NAACP Legal Defense Fund. **© Don Hogan Charles/New York Times Co./Getty Images.**

the university level. In retrospect I would have thought that the elementary and high schools would have moved along like the universities, a little bit at a time the difference being that parents of elementary and high schools are tied to a place of residence, and parents of university students are not. You have people coming from all over to go to a university. But tied to a residence, then you're tied into residential segregation, the whole city-suburb.

So, you think integration would have been more incremental, more gradual?

Mr. Greenberg: Yeah, and by gradual, I mean very gradual. I don't think you can do it all, just because of the residential segregation. I don't see it. Now, the small towns and the rural areas of the country are pretty well integrated because they don't have dense, wide, dense areas of all black and all white.

Since *Brown*, it's all moved off into the political sphere. You're not going to get a court decision saying what you're going to do, you're going to get the Congress, or the state legislature, or the City Council deciding. It's not the same thing with this whole gay marriage thing: The court decided it, now it's all up to the legislatures.

One of things that's clear: There was not a place in the South where a black could get a Ph.D. There was one black medical school. There were no black law schools: Now there are 10,000 black law students. Ole Miss is now well integrated.

> [*Brown*] transformed the particular values of the country. It gave rise to equal rights for women, gays, Hispanics, elderly people, handicapped people.

It transformed the particular values of the country. It gave rise to equal rights for women, gays, Hispanics, elderly people, handicapped people. The whole notion of equality has become pervasive. It transformed the status of black people.

Gilbert Holmes: Certainly it opened the doors. I liked what you said. It opened the doors to people thinking about equality in ways that they really hadn't thought of before, and all the different movements that have sort of spun off it. It certainly opened the door for opportunity. People dreamt about opportunities, but they weren't able to manifest them. I think of my being dean of a law school as the offshoot of *Brown*.

The other side of the legacy is that it also demonstrated how deep-seated some of the racial animus in the country was in terms of the reaction to *Brown*.

Mr. Greenberg: Oh, yeah, the massive resistance.

Mr. Holmes: The massive resistance. And I wouldn't say *Brown* set the stage, but a lot of that resistance did manifest itself with the riots of the '60s and the flight from the urban centers.

Mr. Greenberg: Well you had the riots before the '60s, in the '60s and in the '90s. And there was racial animus before *Brown*, during *Brown* and after *Brown*.

Was anyone surprised by the massive resistance, by the Southern senators and congressmen?

Mr. Greenberg: I was not surprised that the Southern states were opposed to integration, but I was surprised by the violence.

"I was not surprised that the Southern states were opposed to integration, but I was surprised by the violence."

Mr. Holmes: I don't think anybody could have predicted that it would have been that fierce.

Mr. Greenberg: They got up and they argued in the *Brown* case that blacks were inferior, that blacks were diseased, whites wouldn't go to school with them, and things like that. The lawyer from one state said to the court: 'I can tell you that we're never going to send our children to school with black kids.' And (Chief Justice) Warren said, 'I want you to tell me you'll make an honest effort to integrate the schools.' And he said, 'Keep honest out of it.' That's a quote. (laughter) And Warren said, 'No. Put it back in.' You knew there would be resistance, but I didn't think there would be things like Little Rock, or Meredith.[1]

Success was in creating this level of opportunity, this consciousness of racial equality and opportunity that heretofore wasn't present in society?

Mr. Greenberg: No, not at all.

Mr. Holmes: Like I said, the dreams were there, but the manifestations, the manifestations were limited, they were all blocked. So you could say it uncapped the dreams. Would you agree with that Jack, that it uncapped the dreams?

Mr. Greenberg: Oh, yeah. It made things possible. A lot happened. Remember: A black person couldn't get a Ph.D. in the South before 1954.

Resegregation Threatens Opportunity

Talk about resegregation for a moment.

Mr. Holmes: I mention the flight issue because what happens in the cities is that the middle class, predominantly white, and black as well, leave the city and that is what creates the level of segregation in the cities that we have, which is as much economically based as racially based, but has its origins in the lack of opportunity that has been around in this country for centuries, for a very long time.

And the criticism that Brown's *advocates suffered from naiveté?*

Mr. Greenberg: People didn't really expect all the opposition, and didn't even really think about what constituted integration. Marshall talked about just getting the black kids to go to the white schools. And when you stop to think about that, that was not integration? People never really thought about a lot of that. People say, 'what do you think about it, what do you think?' Then you come up with the right answer. But you didn't ask the question. We just wanted to get rid of segregation.

Mr. Holmes: (It was) naiveté, to think it would be a panacea. I think that kind of naiveté is good. I don't take it as a criticism because there was an optimism to it, there was a hope to it. We often want to downgrade naiveté. It's not a bad thing. . . .

One thing that has developed is a large, substantial, effective and prosperous black middle class. That never existed before.

So, what do you see on the horizon?

Mr. Greenberg: Well, I don't know. **One thing that has developed is a large, substantial, effective and prosperous black middle class. That never existed before.** You had the doctor and the lawyer and the undertaker. The lawyers that I knew weren't very prosperous. You had the newspaper publishers like in Baltimore, Carl Murphy. You had the Mitchell family, but that was about it. Now you have quite a substantial black middle class and you've got to balance that off with the unemployed and the low income and the low wealth.

And my favorite statistic—it's not my favorite because I like it, it's my favorite because it's just so striking: A black man in Harlem has the life expectancy of a man in Bangladesh. So, that's the downside.

The upside is that you do have a large number who are going to college and universities and this vibrant middle class.

Mr. Holmes: I agree that there is definitely a vibrant and growing middle class, and the black middle class as a group I think still hasn't figured out how to use the power that it has garnered, the monetary power, the voting power and the like. We still haven't figured that one out, yet. So, 50 years from now, maybe we will have figured that out so that middle class can become a real force for addressing the issues of the lower-income black community. But that to me is the challenge.

Mr. Greenberg: But that assumes that it's going to want to address the challenges of the lower class.

Mr. Holmes: Well I think that to some extent, it may even become necessary . . . the situation with the lower-income black community is such that, like it or not, it reflects on all of the black community. So that the black middle class has a self-interest, although I don't think we have even looked at that. So 50 years from now, it's economics, it's employment. It's much more of those issues, opportunities, to avoid people going into the drug trade and down other paths. And that to me is a bigger challenge because it's harder to identify what to do about it.

Mr. Greenberg: That's right.

Note

1. Note to readers, regarding Meredith: In 1962, African American James Meredith arrived to register at the University of Mississippi. A hostile crowd massed and then rioted; two people died, hundreds were injured. In 1966, as Meredith led a Civil Rights march, he was shot and wounded.

Black Educators in Topeka Adjust to Desegregation

Merrill Ross and Barbara Ann Ross

In the following viewpoint, an African American principal from Kansas discusses his experiences in the aftermath of school integration. He describes four local black schools that had many dedicated teachers as well as community resources that provided support for the educators and the students. He laments that some assumed that books and instruction in black schools were inferior to the resources in the white schools. He also describes the reactions of white teachers and fellow principals after he assumed leadership of an integrated school. In his view, the challenge continues to be getting teachers who are free of prejudice, because educational outcomes depend in great part on their attitudes. He continued to experience racism until he retired, but is grateful that conditions improved

---

SOURCE. Merrill Ross, "Voices of the Era: Merrill Ross," *The Unfinished Agenda of* Brown v. Board of Education, Editors of Black Issues in Higher Education with James Anderson and Dara N. Burne, eds. Hoboken, NJ: John Wiley and Sons, 2004, pp. 80–84.

considerably for all young African Americans. Merrill Ross was an education leader in Topeka, Kansas, and the city's only black principal in 1954, the year *Brown v. Board of Education* was decided. His wife, Barbara Ann, was also a teacher in Topeka. Ross Elementary is named in their honor.

There was great concern for what was going to happen to us as we moved into an integrated curriculum and program. We wondered about whether we would be given consideration according to our level of training. At Washington School our teachers had degrees or levels of training equal to or better than teachers at white schools during that period. That time was a challenge for us because there was no encouragement or invitation for the teachers to be participants in the NAACP's endeavor. The plaintiffs couldn't have realized that the teachers would not be integrated as well. They thought that all of us would be taken in, teachers and pupils. They also hadn't realized that some of the organizations hadn't even tried to look out for us. They had just forgotten us. Maybe they thought we had already been included, but we hadn't.

> "The teachers here were very dedicated, and they prepared those children for things outside."

The teachers weren't moved into the schools very quickly. It was a gradual thing. We felt that once the students were recognized as being very well qualified, then the white parents would ask for the black teachers to come to their schools. Many of the teachers had taught here for a long time. They were up in years and unmarried, they had their roots here. I think they were just hoping and praying that things would work out. They weren't sure that they would be able to go someplace else. They were hopeful for some changes, but they just had to keep quiet and talk among themselves about their concerns.

The Closing of Black Schools

Prior to 1951, there were four black schools: Buchanan School, McKinley School, Monroe School, and Washington School. There was a flood at McKinley School in North Topeka after 1951, and it was closed because of speculation about the condition of the facility. It was sold to a contractor and used as a storage place. Washington School was closed in 1962. After spending sixteen years there, they didn't even put a marker to show where it once existed. This was one of the schools that served black children and they didn't even have that decency.

The teachers here were very dedicated, and they prepared those children for things outside. They knew what was coming. Many of the students who are still living say that they felt good after they were integrated because they didn't feel like they were inferior in any way because of the preparation they received from our teachers. There were a lot of black social clubs where the parents and teachers often came into contact. The sororities and fraternities were all active here. They had forums at the churches in the afternoons, they had resource people in the community who would come to speak to the groups of youngsters and the elderly about health issues to finding jobs. The Washington School teachers made it a point to be as involved with their students as they could. Their students could match up with students from any of the other schools in the city. The teachers made a concerted effort to see to it that no youngster would be left behind. They were continuously encouraged to work hard for what they wanted. We just expected them to do their best.

So many of the people thought that because our children were segregated in the elementary schools that our materials were inferior, that the books were old, or that we didn't have the same books. This was advertised, but it wasn't true. There was a book selection committee with several teachers who were at integrated schools and they brought in materials that were being used in other places. I don't know where they got the idea that our students didn't have the same textbooks, because they did. Some schools may have been older and maybe their books had a little more wear and tear, but there were schools in certain areas where the parents had good jobs and helped to provide what the schools didn't have. The PTA would bring in the materials.

"There were good things that came from desegregation as well as bad things. The outcome depended . . . on the faculties."

Working in an Integrated School System

There were good thing that came from desegregation as well as bad things. The outcome depended in large part on the faculties where the youngsters would be integrating. If the receiving school had a policy whereby all children, according to their skills, talents, and educational outlook would be given just consideration and given an opportunity to be participants, they were easily integrated into the school program without any malice of with any type of prejudices. The fact that the students' reception depended on the training of the white teachers was always disturbing to us at Washington School. Some white teachers were very subtle and made it appear as though color didn't make any difference. Whereas with others, it was rather difficult for them to give a newcomer of a different color the same privileges and the same rights as the other children. Some teachers could be just as open and helpful, while others never could bring themselves around to it.

When Merrill first went to West Avondale, the white school, two teachers were ready to transfer. They had never worked under a black man, and they were not planning on staying there for him to give them instructions. But the board told them that if they couldn't work under him then maybe they had better find work elsewhere. Before the year was up, they were two of Merrill's most staunch supporters because they found out what kind of person he was and what he believed in, what he wanted to do for all the children. Similarly, when the teachers realized that black parents also wanted the best for their children, their attitudes also started to change. On the one hand, because of *Brown* we have a black superintendent, we have black people on the Board of Education who attend to curriculum issues, and we have quite a few of us who are principals. On the other hand, after integration we moved away from the community, schools, homes, and churches that served as the foundation. They prepared our children for the future. **It is still an effort to acquire teachers, qualified teachers, who are free of prejudices. It is part of the American dilemma.**

"It is still an effort to acquire teachers, qualified teachers, who are free of prejudices. It is part of the American dilemma."

There are those individuals who are still subtle in a manner with those prejudices. It wasn't unusual as a child to see a cross burning on the mountain. I also saw men on horseback with the white sheets at about five or six years of age. Today we find ourselves in situations where this kind of racism isn't as obvious. The year before I retired I went to a principals' picnic. I was a little late in getting there, but when I went out on the back porch the white principals were playing Richard Pryor's [1974 comedy album] *That N---r's Crazy*. I didn't say a thing at that time, I tried not to, but I was probably flustered somewhat by the fact that one of them had chosen to play this knowing that I or the other black principals would be there. When September came, I put my name on the agenda for the first principals' meeting. All summer I practiced what I was going to say to them. I remember telling them that at that picnic I was really chagrined and somewhat hurt to think that a group of professional men would resort to what I encountered that day. In my wildest dreams, I had never expected that. I'm sure this wasn't representative of the feeling toward me, but it certainly did not build good relations. I was visibly hurt but I lived through it, and I'm sure that there probably were other occasions like that. It is impossible to screen a person for these subtle forms. There are still many of them that are very subtle and devious in the things they do. Some of our students are able to rise above it and are not affected by it, but it is there in front of them. It's amazing, but for the most part it's not as bad as it used to be for our young people right now.

VIEWPOINT 6

Facing a Mob, an African American Teen Helps Integrate a High School

Minnijean Brown Trickey

In the following viewpoint, a member of the Little Rock Nine describes the frightening experience of integrating Little Rock Central High School in 1957. Shielded by the National Guard, she and the other African American students faced angry crowds outside the school. But inside, the guards couldn't protect her from the petty and cruel racism she was subjected to by her fellow students. She endured the abuse, however, knowing that their efforts were on behalf of all other African American students and in the name of freedom. Minnijean Brown Trickey is an activist who continues to work for social justice. She served as a deputy assistant secretary of the Department of the Interior under US president Bill Clinton and currently works for the Little Rock Central High School National Historic Site.

SOURCE. "Minnijean Brown Trickey, Environmental and Civil Rights Activist," Thirteen/WNET New York, March 26, 2006. Reproduced by permission.

So what happened on that first day of school at Central High?

What happened, for me, was really unexpected. There was a mob. The governor made an announcement on Labor Day that he was going to call in the National Guard, so they were there too. We thought that the National Guard was there to keep the peace, and protect us. So on the first day it was pretty shocking to get there and find out that the Guard were stopping us from going into school. We were sandwiched between the Arkansas National Guard and the mob, so it was quite brutal. I remember shaking. That's the main thing I remember. I remember feeling very scared. And people were screaming obscenities, like 'Go back to Africa' and 'Integration is Communism,' and all kinds of crazy stuff like that. I was totally shocked. I had been a girl of the U.S. who had done all the anthems, songs and pledges, and then I hit that mess and I thought 'Oh my God, this is what it's really like.' In a segregated society you're safe, because you don't do what you're not supposed to do. You didn't do stuff that was against the law, and everything was against the law—buses, trying on clothes, water fountains, restaurants, hotels, swimming pools. So you stayed in your place.

In a segregated society you're safe, because you don't do what you're not supposed to do. . . . You stayed in your place.

So what happened when you got inside the school?

First of all, when we got in on the 24th of September, the mob was quite big, and we were told we had to leave for our own safety. We were taken out secretly through the basement, and it was just scary. So we sat at home for almost 3 weeks, waiting. And we had to go to a federal court, because the school board filed an injunction to delay integration because of the mob and the danger. So we learned quite a lot in that period. Our lawyers were Constance Baker Motley, Thurgood Marshall, and a number of young lawyers in Arkansas. We did all kinds of press conferences. That three weeks was the preparation for what was to happen. By the time we started the first full day at school, we were pretty smart and clear and ready, and we were protected by the 101st Airborne. Lots of things that were to happen later when the 101st left didn't happen on that first day—phone threats, bomb threats in our homes. So we spent those three weeks getting ready for all those crazy people who were behaving as badly as they possible could in every possible way.

> The nine of us just figured, 'This will be rough, let's just go with it.'

What kinds of things did other students do to you, and were the soldiers really able to protect you?

The 101st did protect us, but they couldn't go into the classrooms. I remember walking into the classroom on day one and all these boys had their feet across the aisles. Of course, we were supposed to sit in the back. And I went out to get my guard and the teacher said to him 'No, you don't come in here.' It was just a whole weird experience. They couldn't protect us in the bathroom, so you'd get pushed around in the girls' restroom, in gym—everyone has an incident with hot water in showers and glass on the floor during physical education. So the nine of us just figured, "This will be rough, let's just go with it."

How long did you have to "just go with it"?

The abuse actually escalated over time because the 101st left, and it never ever calmed down. It didn't suddenly become nice, it didn't suddenly become pleasant; it was

Minnijean Brown Trickey stands in front of the school she helped integrate—Central High School in Little Rock, Arkansas—in 2002. © **AP Photo/ Danny Johnston.**

constant. Former students who have done oral histories say they went home every night and practiced what they were going to do the next day to us. I don't think we were protected. In some ways we were better off then than now, because no one thought to kill us right then and there. Although I'm sure they thought about it.

I guess you could say I was a troublemaker, because I tried to say that I should be in the Christmas program, even though we were told we couldn't participate in any activities, other than going to school. That was considered trouble. We were supposed to know our place and act appropriately. So I'm not sure if I was targeted because of that. I have no idea because we [the black students] didn't tell each other what was happening. When you're in the middle of something—I call it "American terrorism at its finest"—you're not sure if you're crazy. We were kids; we weren't sure if things were happening to each other, or if there was some kind of personality flaw that was causing us to be particularly targeted. We were lost in that, just lost in abuse. They threw soup on me a couple of times, and students got up on the lunch table and gave 15 "rahs" for the boy who did it the first time. So for me the abuse was constant, and I have no idea if it was for anyone else.

So how did you get expelled from Central High?

There was a group of 3–5 girls that followed me, stepped on my heels, called me names, spitting at me, just a whole range of harassment. As I was going in my homeroom one morning, these girls threw a purse at me, and I picked it up, and it had six combination locks in it. And I stupidly just dropped it onto the floor and said "Leave me alone, white trash." I didn't keep the purse, so I didn't have any evidence of what happened. That was a good excuse to get rid of me. And after that someone sent around a card that said "One down, eight to go."

Do you regret going to Central High?

No, not at all. That's what we had to do. **We figured out really quickly that this experience was not just about us, it was for everyone**, because of the letters we got from around the world. We had to let everyone know that we were not going to live these isolated and segregated lives. It wasn't pleasant, but it had to be done. I don't regret it.

CHRONOLOGY

1868 The Fourteenth Amendment to the US Constitution is ratified. It guarantees the citizenship of all persons born or naturalized in the United States and provides that "no state shall make or enforce any law which shall abridge the privileges or immunities of citizens of the United States; nor shall any state deprive any person of life, liberty, or property, without due process of law; nor deny to any person within its jurisdiction the equal protection of the laws."

1896 The US Supreme Court upholds segregation in *Plessy v. Ferguson*.

1909 The National Association for the Advancement of Colored People (NAACP) is founded to achieve political, educational, social, and economic equality for all citizens.

1930 The NAACP commissions attorney Nathan Margold to map out a strategy to attack segregation through the court system. Charles Houston, special counsel of the NAACP, decides to pursue "equalization," demanding that equal facilities be established for blacks but stopping short of a direct challenge to *Plessy*.

1938 Thurgood Marshall becomes head of the NAACP legal defense team.

The NAACP team represents Lloyd Gaines, who was denied admission to the University of Missouri law school because of his race. The Supreme Court rules that Missouri must furnish Gaines a legal education within its borders (*Missouri ex rel. Gaines v. Canada*).

1939–1940 Psychologists Mamie and Kenneth Clarke publish research on self-perception of race in young black children. Finding that young black children prefer white dolls to black ones, they conclude that segregation leads to self-hatred in African American children.

1949 Residents of Clarendon County, South Carolina, file *Briggs v. Elliott* with NAACP sponsorship.

1950 The Supreme Court rules that the state of Texas cannot set up an underfunded "black" law school to avoid admitting an African American to the all-white University of Texas law school (*Sweatt v. Painter*).

In *McLaurin v. Oklahoma State Regents*, the court holds that a public institution of higher learning cannot provide inferior treatment to a student because of his or her race.

Thurgood Marshall and the NAACP team decide to pursue a direct attack on *Plessy*.

Bolling v. Sharpe (later consolidated with *Brown*) is filed in Washington, DC.

1951 *Brown v. Board of Education* is filed in district court in Topeka, Kansas.

Davis v. County School Board of Prince Edward County is filed in Virginia.

Gebhart v. Belton is filed in Delaware.

1953 The Supreme Court consolidates the *Brown, Briggs, Davis, Bolling*, and *Gebhart* cases and hears oral argument. Marshall leads the NAACP team, introducing evidence from Clarke's doll studies to argue that segregation harms black children.

Earl Warren becomes chief justice of the Supreme Court.

1954 May 17: The court issues its *Brown v. Board of Education* ruling. Overturning *Plessy v. Ferguson*, the court holds that racial segregation in schools violates the equal protection clause of the Fourteenth Amendment.

1955 May 31: In *Brown II*, the court decrees that desegregation should occur "with all deliberate speed." The statement's vagueness allows the South to avoid desegregating schools.

August 28: Emmett Till, a fourteen-year-old black boy, is murdered after reportedly whistling at a white woman. His funeral draws fifty thousand mourners. Both defendants are acquitted. The case draws extensive media attention and spurs civil rights activism.

December 1: Rosa Parks refuses to give up her bus seat in Montgomery, Alabama, spurring the Montgomery Bus Boycott led by Martin Luther King Jr.

1956 A group of 101 congressmen from the South sign the Southern Manifesto, condemning the *Brown* decision and urging states to resist segregation.

1957 Orval Faubus, governor of Arkansas, deploys the state National Guard to prevent black students from entering Little Rock's previously all-white Central High School. President Dwight D. Eisenhower orders the 101st

Airborne Division of the Army to Little Rock to protect the students.

1959 Prince Edward County, Virginia, closes all of its public schools rather than desegregate them. They remain closed for five years.

1964 Congress passes the Civil Rights Act, barring discrimination in voting, public accommodations, schools, and employment.

1965 The passage of the Voting Rights Act prohibits discrimination in voting.

1967 Thurgood Marshall becomes the first African American appointed to the Supreme Court.

1968 Passage of the Fair Housing Act protects renters and buyers of homes from discrimination in housing.

1969 In *Alexander v. Holmes County Board of Education*, the Supreme Court does away with "all deliberate speed," declaring, "the obligation of every school district is to terminate dual school systems at once and to operate now and hereafter only unitary schools."

1970 The Supreme Court, in *Swann v. Charlotte-Mecklenburg Board of Education*, upholds the use of busing to desegregate, even if the racial imbalance results from students' geographic proximity to schools (*de facto* segregation) rather than intentional (*de jure*) segregation.

1974 The Supreme Court rules that segregation is not remediable unless the districts involved deliberately engaged in segregation (*Milliken v. Bradley*). The decision leads to "white flight" to the suburbs and increasing inner-city segregation.

2007 The court's *Parents Involved in Community Schools v. Seattle School District No. 1* decision declares that public school systems cannot achieve or maintain integration through measures based on a student's race.

FOR FURTHER READING

Books

Jack Balkin, *What* Brown v. Board of Education *Should Have Said: The Nation's Top Legal Experts Rewrite America's Landmark Civil Rights Decision*. New York: New York University Press, 2001.

Melba Patillo Beals, *Warriors Don't Cry: A Searing Memoir of the Battle to Integrate Little Rock's Central High*. New York: Washington Square Press, 1994.

Derrick Bell, *Silent Covenants:* Brown v. Board of Education *and the Unfulfilled Hopes for Racial Reform*. New York: Oxford University Press, 2004.

Adam Fairclough, *Teaching Equality: Black Schools in the Age of Jim Crow*. Athens, GA: University of Georgia Press, 2001.

Ophelia De Laine Gona, *Dawn of Desegregation: J. A. De Laine and Briggs v. Elliott*. Columbia, SC: University of South Carolina Press, 2012.

Jack Greenberg, *Crusaders in the Courts: How a Dedicated Band of Lawyers Fought for the Civil Rights Revolution*. New York: BasicBooks, 1994.

Michael Klarman, Brown v. Board of Education *and the Civil Rights Movement*. New York: Oxford University Press, 2007.

Richard Kluger, *Simple Justice: The History of* Brown v. Board of Education *and Black America's Struggle for Equality*. New York: Vintage, 2004.

J. Anthony Lukas, *Common Ground: A Turbulent Decade in the Lives of Three American Families*. New York: Vintage, 1985.

Waldo Martin, Brown v. Board of Education*: A Brief History with Documents*. Boston: Bedford St. Martins, 1998.

Tim McNeese, Brown v. Board of Education*: Integrating America's Schools* (Great Supreme Court Decisions). New York: Chelsea House, 2006.

Charles Ogletree, *All Deliberate Speed: Reflections on the First Half-Century of* Brown v. Board of Education. New York: Norton, 2004.

James T. Patterson, Brown v. Board of Education*: A Civil Rights Milestone and Its Troubled Legacy*. New York: Oxford University Press, 2001.

Jill Titus, Brown*'s Battleground: Students, Segregationists, and the Struggle for Justice in Prince Edward County, Virginia*. Chapel Hill, NC: University of North Carolina Press, 2011.

Periodicals

"Back Where It Began: School Desegregation," *The Economist*, May 28, 1994.

Jeffrey S. Brooks, "'Integration Was a Solution, but Integration Does Not Address Quality Education': A Conversation About School Desegregation with Dr. Michael A. Middleton," *Teachers College Record*, November 2013, vol. 115, no. 11.

Koda Borgelt-Mose and Tammy Johnson, "Beyond Brown; Snapshots of a New Era in Education," *Colorlines*, 7.2, Summer 2004.

Kevin Chappell, "Topeka 50 Years Later: The Real Story Behind the Brown in *Brown v. Board*," *Ebony*, May 2004, vol. 59, no. 7.

Adam Cohen, "The Supreme Struggle," *New York Times*, January 18, 2004.

Adam Fairclough, "The Costs of Brown: Black Teacher and School Integration," *Journal of American History*, June 2004, vol. 91, no. 1.

Mary Hatwood Futrell and Joel Gomez, "How Tracking Creates a Poverty of Learning," *Educational Leadership*, May 2008, vol. 65, no. 8.

Jack Greenberg, "*Brown v. Board of Education*: An Axe in the Frozen Sea of Racism," *Dissent*, Fall 2004, vol. 51, no. 4.

Lawrence Hardy, "A New Minority, 50 Years After Brown," *Education Digest*, September 2004, vol. 70, no. 1.

Katy June-Friesen, "Massive Resistance in a Small Town," *Humanities*, September/October 2013, vol. 34, no. 5.

Michael J. Klarman, "It Could Have Gone the Other Way," *Nation*, May 3, 2004, vol. 278, no. 17.

James E. Lyons and Joanne Chesley, "Fifty Years After *Brown*: The Benefits and Tradeoffs for African American Educators and Students," *Journal of Negro Education*, Summer 2004, vol. 73, no. 3.

Martha Minow, "*Brown v. Board* in the World: How the Global Turn Matters for School Reform, Human Rights, and Legal Knowledge," *San Diego Law Review*, Winter 2013, vol. 50 no. 1.

Alan Richard, "The Heat of Summerton," *Nation*, May 3, 2004, vol. 278, no. 17.

Paul Craig Roberts and Lawrence M. Stratton Jr., "Color Code," *National Review*, vol. 47, no. 5, March 20, 1995, p. 36.

Cass Sunstein, "Did *Brown* Matter?," *New Yorker*, May 3, 2004, p. 10.

Websites

The Brown Foundation for Educational Equity, Excellence and Research (http://brownvboard.org). The website of the Brown Foundation, which was founded by the family of the late Oliver Brown, features a number of multimedia resources about the history and impact of the *Brown v. Board of Education* trial and about the foundation's scholarships and other education programs.

***Brown v. Board of Education* National Historic Site, Kansas** (www.nps.gov/brvb). The National Park Service operates the site of the former Monroe Elementary School as a park that celebrates the end of racial segregation in the United States. In addition to facts about visiting the historic site, the website includes information about the five cases decided in *Brown v. Board of Education*, and many educational resources for teachers and students.

***Brown v. Board of Education:* Virginia Responds** (www.lva.virginia.gov/exhibits/brown). This companion website of an exhibition at the Library of Virginia provides information on the Virginia lawsuit that became part of the landmark school integration case and presents a wealth of original documents that expose the diverse local reactions to school integration in Virginia.

NAACP Legal Defense and Educational Fund, "Landmark: *Brown v. Board of Education*" (www.naacpldf.org/case/brown-v-board-education). The website of the organization that led the legal fight for school integration in the United States has background information on the case and reflections on its legacy, as well as access to information on other LDF cases and current activities.

Southern School Desegregation, 1957–1962 (www.pbs.org/wgbh/amex/eyesontheprize/story/03_schools.html). *Eyes on the Prize: America's Civil Rights Movement, 1954–1985* is a multimedia project of the Public Broadcasting System (PBS). This section explores—with explanatory text, contextual press clippings, music and video clips, and maps—the events and people of the era of school integration in the United States.

'With an Even Hand': *Brown v. Board* at Fifty (www.loc.gov/exhibits/brown/brown-aftermath.html). This section of the Library of Congress website provides access to a number of historic documents in the library's collection related to the history of school integration in the United States.

INDEX

T

U

V

W